© 2023 Jude Gorini

The Colourblind Grief

All rights reserved. No part of this publication may be reproduced, stored in a retrieval system or transmitted in any form or by any means, electronic, mechanical, photocopying, recording or otherwise without the prior permission of the publisher or the author of the relevant work who retains the copyright of his work in accordance with the provisions of the Copyright, Designs and Patents Act 1988 or under the terms of any license permitting limited copying issued by the Copyright Licensing Agency.

ISBN: 978-1-7394044-0-6

Published by Experiments in Fiction
www.experimentsinfiction.com

Jude Gorini

THE COLOURBLIND GRIEF

THE COLOURBLIND GRIEF

JUDE GORINI

TO ANDREA

— JUDE GORINI

Contents

Hurricane Drunk	13
Long & Lost	23
What the Water Gave Me	36
Various Storms & Saints	48
My Boy Builds Coffins	59
Seven Devils	69
Light of Love	75
Ghosts	96
Mother	110
Heaven is Here	121
Cosmic Love	140
Ship to Wreck	159
Kiss with a Fist	169
I am Daniel	182
Acknowledgements	197

Daniel,

I am not sure if you will ever read this letter and, knowing how proud you are, probably you will tear it up and throw it somewhere. But I want to be positive about it, and hopefully you are reading it, right now. I don't know how many days I have left. Some doctors say months, others, years, but as far as I feel, I don't think I have much time left. And this is one of the reasons I want to apologise to you and not leave this heaviness that keeps ruining both of our lives.

I know I've made many mistakes and one of them was the communication between us, and how I was not honest about who we were. But now I want to ask you to put yourself in my position. No one ever explained to me how to be a mother, and the only example I had was your grandmother. My childhood was full of responsibilities, and already from a really young age I had to work to provide food for the family. The only type of love I received from my mother was a slap in the face, every time I did not cook the food in the way she wanted. I had a hell of a childhood, but you already know that.

When I knew I was pregnant with you, I was so happy. One of the promises I made was to never repeat the mistakes my mother made with me, and to really love you, giving my entire life to you. But all this wasn't easy for many reasons, including the way life pushes you to always be perfect without making any mistakes. I think I wasn't a bad mother to you at all. I tried to give you all the love and options you needed. Even if sometimes I was harsh or heartless to you, that was my way to push you to be the best version of yourself. Did that work? I think it did.

Life is hard, and for me it was, and is, the most difficult challenge I face each day. I am a victim of the circumstances around me and living with that makes me choose the hardest path most of the time, enabling me to be strong, both as a woman and mother. As I said, I don't know how much time I have left, but I will ask you to do a couple of things for me. Take care of Paloma, your sister. She doesn't know how to live life, and doesn't know the meaning of choices. Without me, she will be lost, and I am sure that if you stay next to her, she will gain the confidence that I can see in you. You think she doesn't love you, but it is not like that, she adores you so much. So please help her to be a better version of herself.
I want to be cremated and please, throw my ashes into the ocean, which is the only place that I belong.

As much as we don't communicate anymore as we used to, I want to tell you something: Daniel, I am the luckiest mother on earth to have you. I know I hurt you so many times, but I am sure that deep in your heart you love me as much as I love you.

I am proud of you and always will be.

Your dearest Mother

Hurricane Drunk

I don't even know how many times I have written my story repeatedly. I always have that sense of fear that emerges when you are afraid of letting people know the real truth about you. We are so afraid of being judged, that most of the time, it is better to stay in the corner of our life saying nothing. Feeling invisible can be one of the best emotions someone can live with.

But this time, I want to start it all differently. I want to tell you what happened to me, and what I went through in order to be here, sitting on this old scratchy desk writing and watching the sunrise over this immense ocean that keeps giving me the opportunity to be free.

I am Daniel; a 35-year-old Latino queer man with an uncured mental disorder. Crazy, isn't it?

Yes, crazy as the train of thoughts that follow me each second of my life.

But let me explain where it all started. In early 2011, I made the decision that I needed a change of place and air. I was living in Madrid at that time. In January that year, I had a horrible break up that left me in pieces and lost. The person I was with was a drug addict. Our life together was just a mess, to the point I started taking drugs with him just for the sake of pleasing him with his wrong life choices. But that kind of life and relationship couldn't last forever, especially once we started to be an open couple with someone new in our bed each day. When you are high, that is OK, but when you are back to sobriety, paranoia and sadness kicks you in your teeth, and that hurts. That snowy January, I decided to leave him. On his side, though, the best way to stop it all was to tell everyone around us that I was the drug addict, and that in those 3 years together, I had ruined his life, emotionally and economically. People around us didn't want to be part of that drama, so they listened to just one side of the story. Because of that, I lost many of them. I went back to live with my mother, her husband, and my step-sister Paloma. They lived in the middle of Spain, in a little village called Torre Baja, two hours journey from Valencia. That was a horrible choice also, because rumours of my "drug addiction" had reached my mother, and she tried to take me to many doctors and potential rehab places:

'I don't want our family to know we have an addict, do you know the shame we will pass through if they know that?' she kept repeating daily, touching her heart as if she was having a heart attack. She was a classic Latino drama queen, all about her and her judgemental thoughts. I couldn't cope with that situation, so I saved all the money I could, put my things into an 'American Tourister' suitcase, and went to London. I left family and friends behind, hoping to find money, stability and, most importantly of all: Love. I already knew a few people in London, and Janice, a friend that moved there years before, gave me her sofa for two weeks until I could find a house or a room of my own. And that was challenging, mostly because many landlords wanted references that were impossible to obtain, since I had never lived in the UK before. After ten days of crashing on Janice's sofa, I found a room in Stratford through a friend of a friend. The landlord demanded 4 months' deposit paid in advance, without giving me the opportunity to check the room first.

At that moment, I didn't have much choice, so I found myself in the filthiest house I had ever lived in, with 9 flatmates. It was an old Victorian house. My room had once been the living room. The walls were full of mould, and the window was half-broken:

'I promise I will fix the window, but for the moment let's use some tape.' Mario, the landlord, said, with a smirk on his face. Fortunately, the same week, someone came to change the window, and I had to paint the walls with an anti-mould paint. It took me one week to professionally clean the dirty room, the kitchen and the bathroom, something no one in that house had ever done before. There was no cleaning rota in there, something I introduced quickly, and to which my flatmates took happily, since none of them wanted to live in that disgusting state anymore. I didn't have a lot of savings, so I had to find a job as soon as possible. One April morning, I went to open a new bank account in Lloyds bank, and to the Job Centre in Whitechapel to obtain my National Insurance number. For the first time, I faced the difficulty of understanding different English accents. I started learning English when I was a little child, probably 5. My mother wanted me to speak fluently by the age of eight, something that happened, but the only problem was that my teacher spoke American English with a strong Spanish accent: something that became mine, too. Speaking with foreigners was fine, but when I had to face a proper British person, things were trickier, firstly, because of the quick way people spoke, and secondly, because of the different accents they had. The Job Centre office lady was a tall blonde woman from Scotland, and when she started to ask me questions in order to fill out the form, I felt I couldn't understand anything. But in the end, I got my National Insurance number, which meant I could start searching for jobs. Even if my studies were in Marketing and Accountancy, I applied for any job I could find, from Bartender to Junior Marketing Specialist. The people I knew in London kept saying how easy and quick it would be to find a job:

'Next year the Olympics will be here, and so many places are looking for staff already: it will be easy.' That was the same conversation I heard all the time in front of a pint of 'Camden Hells,' the best beer ever. It was July, and after almost four months in London, I still had no job. I started to worry, since I only had enough money to survive another month. I was already surviving on digestive biscuits and milk. Then, on a night out paid by the German twink flatmate I had, I met a British man. His name was Nigel, he was from Nottingham and had been living in London for the last 8 years. He worked in the Marketing department of a fashion brand. We talked all night, and we ended naked in his bedroom for the entire Sunday. Between sex, cuddling, and food, he shared my CV with his HR department.

The following Tuesday, I was called for an interview, and after 3 hours, I was hired, and started work the following Monday. I was more of a Junior Assistant than a Junior Marketing Specialist, but it was fine: the money was enough to pay my rent and food, and that was perfect. Nigel and I dated for a while. At work, we pretended to be colleagues, even when we ran into the toilet together for a quickie. But it all ended when Nigel told me that his boyfriend was back in town, and he couldn't be there for me anymore. I was in shock, but not very surprised, since it wasn't the first time I'd been in a relationship where I was the lover, and not the lucky boyfriend.

I started to learn more about British culture, slang and the London accent.In September, I moved to a new house in Bethnal Green, shared with 3 perfect strangers: Nicola and Naomi from Manchester, and Matteo from Italy. My room was quite spacious, with big windows looking towards Weavers Field Park. The house was newly refurbished, and thankfully my flatmates had cleaning O.C.D. issues. It was paradise.

In September, our Saturdays were about watching X-Factor, going for a pint in The Old George pub, then taking the bus to Dalston to go clubbing. Sundays, in contrast, were all about hangovers: going for a Sunday roast and returning home to see X-Factor: The Results. We all supported Little Mix, who won the show in the end: we went to see them live in Heaven, what an experience! As much as we shared many times together and talked about all the superficial stuff, in the end we didn't know much about each other. They didn't have a clue that I was living through a huge depression 90% of the time, punctuated by high moments of hypomania.

In the meantime, I dated many guys that I met through Gayromeo, or simply sitting in Caffè Nero in Soho. I loved the fact that I could have a man from any part of the world. We were all in the same situation: Pretending we were looking for love, when really we were just interested in having wild sex.

My real problems started on a chilly day in London. I was 25. It was December 2011, a few weeks before Christmas. I'd just had my birthday in November, which makes me a Scorpio with a second sign in Libra: the weakest link.

I was born and raised in a Brazilian environment, where it is built into your DNA to think:

'To survive in this world; you need money. You need to show up as what you are not. Always being the centre of attention, and pretending to be the strongest person on this earth. And if you feel weak, keep quiet and pretend everything is OK. In the end, God or Jesus will help you, somehow.'

It is insane how, in my culture, we use God in each step of our life experience. Pray God, thank God, God is with you, God is with us. When I was little, I was afraid to do anything.

I felt this heaviness of God watching all of my steps:

'God sees what you are doing, behave' is a classic Latino Mother sentence; a perfect way to make you feel ashamed of your own steps.

Even if God was watching me, at seven years old, I was already attracted to my male schoolmates, and I would imagine being their wife. My idea of a relationship was crazy: I was the wife, and they the awful husband asking me to do laundry, or anything connected to the housewife experience. In my teenage years, I would touch myself, imagining having hardcore sex with any man I had around me. And when I say *any* man, I mean it. I had big masturbation moments thinking of the old priest from our church.

Yes, I was perverse.

But I could still feel this heaviness above my head, of God watching over and judging me.

Once, I tried to sell my soul to Satan. At least, I thought that was the way. I wrote on a piece of paper: 'Satan, take my soul, and in exchange I want a pair of tits, and money.' I remember waking up the day after, looking at my chest, hoping to find huge breasts, but nothing of that sort happened. Instead, I got mental health issues: hyperactivity, hypomania, and depression that I dealt with alone for many years. From that episode, I might have realised that there was something not right in my mind, but living in a family where

I was expected to just be a 'strong man' with no weaknesses, I lived with it all as though it were something normal. And, not having anyone to tell about it, I genuinely thought we were all crazy as fuck. Without realising it was happening, my mental health was already breaking me. I was clearly naive for being OK with it: I used to live in self-destruction mode most of the time.

But on that wintry day, London had something magical in store for me.

Christmas lights were everywhere, Christmas songs were coming out of stores, and many people on the Tube were wearing Christmas jumpers. I supposed most of them were going to a Christmas party, or else they simply loved Christmas as much as I hated it. I had never had a great love for Christmas time. Mainly because my mother told me when I was three years old, 'Listen, I am Santa Claus, so choose your gift and I will buy it.'

That day, I was walking along the Thames, going towards Tower Bridge. This was the only place that made me feel I was really living in London. I could smell cinnamon coming from a few little market stalls selling mulled wine, and hear kids screaming out loud on the carousel. The sky was clear, and there was a light breeze caressing my face. I wore a Burberry vintage coat found in Camden market for a few pounds, bought in the place where Amy Winehouse used to work before she got famous.

Everything was beautiful and magical, except the way I was feeling inside. I had this turmoil breaking me: something was off, and I didn't want to deal with it. I felt my heart pounding, and thoughts going in all directions, to the point that I felt lost. I was gasping for breath.

'Are you OK, mate?' a tourist asked me while I was bending towards the floor. Was I OK? No, I wasn't. I just wanted to scream and finish my life at that moment, but instead I nodded, saying, 'All OK, just hurt my leg. I am becoming old, haha! I will sit down, thanks.' He left me there, turning his face to me and shaking his head. I think he thought I was high on something: I wished I was.

I spent the rest of that morning sitting on the steps, watching over Tower Bridge on Queen's Walk, with thousands of people passing in front of me, taking pictures and videos of that magnificent tower. What was happening to me? Why could I suddenly not face the fact I was alive? Why did I feel the urge to end my life? Many times, the idea of dying passed through my mind. I imagined how my funeral would be, how many people would be there in mourning, and how many of them would cry or say something such as, 'Daniel was a great fella, and we will all miss his smile and laugh.'

The day passed quickly. In the afternoon, I stood up from where I was seated and took the DLR to Shadwell, where I had a bite to eat and three bottles of wine, the only medicine that was recommended by my mother:

'If you are feeling down, drink and all will be perfect.' She would tell me. My mother and I were both sad drinkers. I never understood why I followed her advice, but supposedly there was something cultural about drinking and being sad, turning everything into craziness, and the next day forgetting everything with a terrible hangover to further mess with the mind.

Eventually, I went back home with tears falling down my face. I was alone. All my flatmates were working. So I sat in the living room, took my phone and started scrolling through my Facebook feeds. Funhouse Daniel was my name there, a huge dedication to Pink's album Funhouse, the album that helped me go through the break-up I had had a few months before. And while I was drinking, I kept stalking the feed page of my ex-boyfriend, before going through the feeds of all the friends who were not talking to me anymore to me because of him. I cried.

That room and phone were too much for me, so I stood up, took my crystal wine glass, bought at TK Maxx Clearance in Hackney, and decided that the next glass would be the last of my life. I went into my bedroom, taking with me a blister of Xanax that a friend of mine had given me as a birthday gift, 'use it if you feel anxious,' they'd said. I took four, and drank them with my last glass of wine, then left the house and sat by a bench in Weavers Field. That is the last thing I remember.

Long & Lost

Waking up in a hospital and not having a clue what has happened is more nerve-wracking than dealing with something you don't want to deal with, but you have to: that is life.

'Mr Piriz (It is Perez), welcome back. You are in the Royal London hospital. You were taken here by ambulance yesterday. Today we will have to do a couple of exams to see if everything is OK, and later the psychiatrist will come to have a chat with you. Nothing to be worried about, just part of the whole process,' said the tall black doctor, smiling at me while behind him a nurse kept shaking her head in disapproval, which only added to my feelings of guilt and shame.

'OK' was the only word that came out of my mouth. What have I done? Why am I here? Why? How? What? I was so shocked that I couldn't speak. Did I really manage to attempt suicide? Was I really in that darkness?

All these questions ran through my mind until the psychiatrist came to visit me and explained: 'You attempted suicide, and for this reason, we will need to go through a process to make sure you do not harm yourself anymore.'

The next few weeks were some of the most challenging I have ever lived through. I went back home a few days later, but I had to go back each day to do tests and assessments.

My flatmates were gone for the Christmas holidays. They had had a Christmas dinner together, and because I hadn't been there with them, they left me a card which said:

'Have a great Xmas, we are next to you, and stay safe. Love you, crazy Latino.'

'Crazy and alone' was the best way to describe how I felt at that moment. I took a few sick days from work, using the excuse that I had a stomach bug to get rid of. No one knew what had happened, and I was terribly ashamed to share it. I was afraid of being judged and having people say, 'I am sorry, what can I do for you?' During those days, I had thousands of calls from my mother and sister, which all went unanswered. I didn't want to hear their voices, but eventually, I had to call back.

'Hey family, I am fine. Yes… yes… sorry. It was a stomach bug. Yes, I am fine. No, no, don't come here. I am fine. Yes, Merry Christmas.' I kept gasping for words, while my mother screamed angrily on the other side of the receiver. She was afraid, and disappointed because I hadn't answered any calls or messages. She told me they had been ready to come and contact the police in order to find out where I was, though this was something I knew she would never do. She only cared about herself, and not about me.

I just felt awfully guilty for the entire Christmas period, playing back and forth in my mind the reasons why I really wanted to end my life, and why I had been so stupid as to attempt it. I had mostly everything I wanted in life. Yes, I wanted love, too, but everything else was fine. This was still not enough to put my mind at rest. A few days after Christmas, my GP called me and said:

'Daniel, can you come here tomorrow morning? We have to talk about the results of your assessments and tests.'

That morning, I woke up with a heaviness in my heart that was screaming, 'God is judging you.' That voice changed while walking to my GP. I started to feel a strange happiness and a voice in my mind saying, 'you are OK, and the doctor will say everything is fine.' I was afraid he would confirm I was mentally ill, or had long term health complications. That idea made me crazy while sitting in the waiting room full of people talking loudly. Then my turn arrived, and the doctor sat in front of me asking how I was feeling, then continued:

'After all the assessments and tests you took, I have to tell you something about your mental health. Often, we don't understand why our mind tends to complicate situations and make us do strange things. Did you ever feel, during your normal day, a change in your mood and your perception of reality?'

I nodded.

'And how did you feel about it?' he asked, clicking on his pen, ready to write something down on my medical record.

'I don't know. I always lived with that, and I thought everyone else lived with it too. I am OK, even if sometimes it is challenging,' I said, looking at my hands, which were shaking more than ever before. 'OK, Daniel. After all the tests and assessments, we can give a name to this way of living life. You suffer from bipolar disorder one, and that means…'At that moment, all I could hear was, 'Blah, blah, blah,' how in the hell I was bipolar? A voice in my mind kept screaming, 'liar!' So I stopped him and said, 'Impossible. Everyone lives in this way, with the same run of thoughts. Everyone is hyperactive, happy and depressed in the same day, what are you talking about? Are you trying to say that I am crazy?' He looked at me with empathy and said, 'No, Daniel, I am not calling you crazy. You have a mental illness that we can cure using a combination of psychotherapy and medication. People that are not bipolar are quite balanced when we talk about dealing with emotion, life experience and more, and we want you to achieve that. So we will start with this mood balance….'

'Fuck!' I was astonished by the fact I was mentally insane, after thinking my whole life that I was fine. This changed my life.

Months passed with me living through different medications and therapists. In the first three months, I had to change drug therapy probably three or four times. The side effects were lots of fun! I had nausea most of the time, and I had to run to the loo many times during the day. I felt bloated and confused. But one of the side effects I loved the most was feeling numb. I felt devoid of emotion towards my life and the world around me. It was such a strange high sensation. It is difficult to describe. I was mostly staring at things for hours and letting it all go by quickly. I think, at that moment, that if someone died in front of me, I would just call an ambulance and be OK with it. My life seemed like a movie, no longer like reality. The doctor recommended that I stay away from alcohol and drugs, something which was quite difficult, but I respected it. I wanted to be normal as quickly as possible.

At work, no one noticed anything. I seemed more focused on everything, and my superior kept giving me compliments about my professionalism, and how happy the company was about me. During the leaving party for my colleague, Christine, we all went out for dinner. I sat in the corner, no drinks for me, just sparkling water. This left a few of my colleagues shocked, since they knew I was a good drinker. The confusion there was insane. There was too much information to take in, and my mind was totally numbed. When Christine stood up and started her speech, many were crying. Instead, I was staring at the wall behind her and swaying. I felt no emotion, and I was swaying so much that Mary, my desk colleague, came and asked:

'Daniel, are you OK darling? Are you high?'

'No, Mary, don't be stupid. I am not feeling well, I have to go. Say goodbye to everyone for me,' I said, while grabbing my things and leaving the party.

The days passed, and finally the new treatment started working. I was not feeling numb anymore, I seemed more balanced, and I also managed to find a hot Irish therapist to comfort and help me through the process.

'Daniel, it is important we focus step by step in this journey, and every little step is a giant step, so be proud of yourself and your growth,' the hot therapist said in our first session together, while in my mind, I dreamed of having sex with him. A tall man with long ginger hair in a bun, with a long beard and a strong Irish accent that made him my only God in that messy world. During our sessions, I couldn't focus much. I kept nodding in a flirty way. I just wanted to be fucked on that desk.

My treatment journey was going according to plan. The medicines were opening up my mind, making things clearer. I felt more balanced in my emotions, and open to my vulnerability. I had a hot therapist from Dublin and received a promotion at work, but outside of that bubble I was alone. No partners, no friends (at least so I thought), no fun, no sex, no weekends out dancing. Nothing. I was getting unconsciously hard on myself; I didn't want to break any rules. I liked that mind normality. And as much as I was tempted to break it all, I felt strong enough to keep following the treatment plan.

People that were around me knew nothing about what was happening, my flatmates were inspired by my sobriety, which I sold as a spiritual journey of self-learning, rather than mental health issues that had come to light as a result of an attempted suicide. But then my flatmates left our home one by one for new job opportunities outside London, leaving me there in charge of everything, including interviewing for new flatmates, whom I eventually found. We were now a household of four gay international guys.

I was feeling terribly alone, and that loneliness was tough for me. But this was a topic I never shared with my therapist. I felt I didn't want to sound as miserable as I was already feeling since the attempted suicide. So I lied, talking about having days out with imaginary friends in places I had never really been. And I also played a Brazilian game my mother taught me:

'If you feel bad and weak, pretend everything is fine, and never show your weakness to anyone.' So, I pretended everything was fine, and that I was strong enough to deal with something that was unreal.

I joined morning yoga classes in Shoreditch House, thanks to a colleague who managed to give me membership. Shoreditch house is a sort of membership club with many events and things to do, including a rooftop pool and other facilities. That process was insanely difficult. I had to have 2 signatures and letters from 2 members of the house assuring them I was a great person, into The Arts (or whatever) to be part of the house. Even if the process was quite fast and smooth, I felt as if I was selling my soul to Shoreditch house. It was a nice place to be, plus, on Sundays they had different promotions for members: a great way to save money in an expensive environment. But then my life shifted, and something happened.

It was a warm day in April. Normally, in London at that time of year, you have very little warm weather, but 2012 was different: we had a proper summer week. Supposedly it was a message from Mother Nature, saying, 'I can't wait for the Olympics, so let me give you all an early summer week.' Everyone was out: going to the park in t-shirts, shorts and sunglasses. Even though I lived in front of a park, I started to hang out in Victoria Park. Weavers' field was too traumatic for me, since I had passed out there on a bench.

Mornings after yoga, I walked in the park, which was busy with people running, and others enjoying a coffee by the little lake. In my bag, I carried *Mrs Dalloway* by Virginia Woolf, one of my favourite books, and I always had my earphones on, listening to music.

In Victoria Park, there is a bar called the Pavilion Café by the tiny lake looking towards green island and the Chinese Pagoda, something that I still find incongruous in that majestic park. That day, I sat there with my sunglasses on, and a voice behind me said, 'Daniel, are you pretending not to see me?' I turned my head, confused. I could be a cold-hearted bitch, but I always said 'hi,' even to those I didn't like. In front of me there was Jacob, the first date I had had when I moved to London.

He was a tall blonde guy from Bristol, with beautiful plump lips and freckles on his nose. We met through the gayromeo website, the best place to find someone at that time. After a long online exchange about everything and nothing, we went on a date. He was extremely sweet and funny, something that bothered me a lot, though I wasn't sure why. I felt as though that behaviour was fake, but then I learned that it is just a British way to get to know someone. But at the time, I thought that sweetness was his card to take me to his bed, which he could do anyway, even without all that smoochy cheesy stuff. 'OMG, Jacob…wow, sorry I had my head in the clouds. Wow! Come sit here. How are you?' I said, smiling, realising how handsome he was, something I hadn't realised on our first date. 'Oh, thank you, sure I am not bothering you?' He asked. I touched his hand, saying, 'Don't be stupid.' 'I really thought you didn't want to say hi. You know, we never saw each other after that date, and you never answered me back, so I thought I had done something bad to you.' He said, while softly squeezing my hand.

I always had that strange approach to dates. People that were clearly interested in me were those I would be ghosting strictly after the date, and those who I liked were those ghosting me. And in that case, I would be a mad stalker, searching for and bothering them for weeks upon weeks. With Jacob, it was me ghosting him. I knew he liked me a lot, but in my mind, it was senseless for someone to like me. I had trust issues, and, as much as I wanted to be loved, I was picky when choosing from whom I wanted to receive love.

I grew up without any lessons in how to love someone. My mother kept saying throughout my childhood that she loved me, but it was just her way of manipulating my mind any time she wanted me to leave the room she was in. For most of my childhood, I grew up without a male role model. My father died of a heart attack in Spain at the beginning of my mother's pregnancy. My mother returned to Brazil to give birth, and the first male figure I had in my life was when I was 13 years old. His name is Jose, the new husband of my mother, and my step-father. I hated him from the outset, but there was nothing I could do, so I had to deal with it.

In all my love relationships, I had looked for a father figure, someone who needed to be tough, strong and powerful. But in all my dates and relationships, the men I was with were too balanced, calm and sweet, (apart from the crazy drug addict I had been with), clearly not my cup of tea at all! 'Oh, Jacob, that was almost 1 year ago! Let's forget about it! I was new to London, and everything was crazy. So, tell me how are you doing? Have you found love?' I said, while double squeezing his hands. 'Oh yes, 1 year ago, wow time flew, didn't it? Yes, that's OK, no worries, I forgive you.' We laughed, building that flirting energy between us. 'Oh no, single as ever. You know how it is in London, mostly everyone looking for fun. Would you like to drink something? Let's have a pint, no?'

He looked at me, smiling, while in my mind the word 'pint' came as an explosion.

'Yes sure, if they have Camden Hells or Fosters,' I said confidently, while many voices in my head kept saying, 'No, you can't drink…yes you can… no, that is not the rule. Well, it's OK, a pint won't kill me.'

I smiled at Jacob while he walked to the bar. In my mind, I started making peace with myself, saying out loud, 'That's OK, it is one pint and nothing will happen.' I felt as if my demons were there, sitting with me, ready to see the mess I would make, mixing my medication with alcohol. For a moment, I felt like my mother when she used to take alprazolam with vodka. Jacob came back with that big hot smile and gave me my pint. We raised our glasses and started chatting, sharing our news from the past year, with me leaving out my mental illness and attempted suicide. He talked about many dates he had had, how awful they were, and how tiring the London dating life was for someone as romantic as him. I laughed and took the mickey out of him, saying, 'Mate, how can a Bristolian be romantic?' He laughed, putting his hands on his face and shaking his head. I told him about my promotion and my membership of Shoreditch House, adding that we should go together for Sunday drinks. We raised our glasses again, and I silently cheered for my first drink in months. That pint felt divine. I could already feel a strange tingling sensation running through my body and mind. Second sip, and my mind was lightheaded with all inhibition gone. A third long sip, and I was completely drunk, babbling words and laughing. But the conversation went on and on, sharing deep drunk ideas and opinions about the Queen's Jubilee and how the Olympics would mess up the Central Line; the growth of Stratford, and the many new stores opening around town. How Brick Lane was full of bloggers and fashion students on Sundays, waiting to be photographed, and how both of us were feeling alone despite the town constantly growing and booming. It was 1pm, and he asked, 'Would you like to come to mine? We can drink and have something to eat. I can cook superb carbonara?' I nodded happily, glad to be spending the day with someone at last. I felt I could fly above the clouds that were fogging my life at that moment. 'I just hope it is not a British carbonara with ham!' I teased him. 'If my grandmother had wheels, she would have been a bike.' He said with an Italian accent, copying the Gino d'Acampo moment from the 'This Morning' TV show. We left, laughing, and he placed his arm around my shoulder while walking to his house. He lived in an open space in front of the Buddhist temple in Mile End. He worked in Finance, earned good money, and had the entire space to himself. He took a bottle of cheap white wine and gave me the opener. He started to move things around the kitchen and said, 'I have a bunch of vinyls there, choose what you like and put it on.' There were many artists in his collection, including Lianne La Havas' Album, 'Is your love big enough?'

'You know, I once met Lianne la Havas outside the Arts Club in Dover street: such a tiny, beautiful girl with a guitar. I was too shy to say hi, but I smiled at her, and she smiled back at me.' I said while putting her vinyl on.

'That is a story, I like her. Such a fresh artist, this is what we need more in music,' he screamed, while putting the boiler on for the pasta.

While he was cooking the carbonara, the music started, and I put on the track 'Lost & found,' still one of my favourite songs of hers. With my glass of wine in my hand, I started to dance. I felt drunk. Sadness was kicking me. I sat down and started to cry. As much as I was feeling lightheaded and drunk, I could feel my heart squeezing and exploding into thousands of pieces. 'You are a fucking mess,' my mind told me. Jacob left what he was doing and came to hug me:

'Hey, hey, are you OK? It is all fine. Come here.' His hug was strong and firm, which was what I really needed in those lonely weeks. 'Hey, look at me, everything is fine, OK?' I looked into his eyes and kissed his plumply soft lips. I had never felt so sad and good at the same time in my entire life.

That kiss was passionate, and I took off his shirt and kissed his neck. He took me to the sofa. I allowed the music, alcohol, and my antidepressants to do their work. I needed love and appreciation, and he was there giving it to me. 'Unfold me and teach me to be like somebody else,' Lianne sang, while we pleasured ourselves. I was happy, I was sad, I was confused. I was drunk. I was mentally insane.

What the Water Gave Me

The relationship with Jacob continued for a couple of months, or maybe less than that. He was totally unaware of what was going on with my mental health. I was too ashamed to talk about it. I felt I would ruin our relationship, and he would escape from me, something I couldn't cope with, but eventually had to deal with. In the last weeks together, I just started to go mental about everything, and had many moments of crying in which he would leave and say something like, 'Listen, I'm going to leave you alone with your drama.' The hidden abuse of alcohol and medicines was out of control, to the point I no longer understood what was real, and what was part of my sick mind. I just wanted to be loved and accepted by him. In our last moments together, I got over-dramatic about the fact he didn't remember our monthly anniversary. I screamed the worst possible abuse against him, and all this in front of many witnesses in a pub. His face was so disappointed by my behaviour that he stood up and said, 'Mate, you need to see a doctor because you are fucking crazy,' and left me there in tears, while people looked at me as though I were insane, which, at that moment, I was. After that conversation, we broke up, or better, we ghosted out from our life together, and I started with a new relationship that became as toxic as hell, as it involved alcohol and medicines. Each evening after work, I bought a bottle of wine or cheap vodka that I mixed with my pills. That became the only moment I felt free from the hellish reality in which I was living. The situation became out of control to the point that I was sneaking drugs and alcohol everywhere I went. I preferred to be alone during the process of getting high and fucked, watching the white walls of my room and crying. People around me were constantly inviting me for drinks, lunches, dinners, and I would mostly say, 'I am sorry, I am really busy with work and other things, let's plan for next week,' and that next week would never happen. My bottle of drinkable alcohol and pill were my best friends now. I felt they could understand me better than any other human.

Meanwhile, London was booming. Two months before the beginning of the Olympics, there were events taking place everywhere. Concerts, festivals, workshops, and new places to visit like the Olympic Park, but I preferred to stay in my room, getting high and crying my eyes out.

How could I cheat my addiction by spending time talking about Rihanna in Hackney's big weekend, or the Lovebox line up? I was out of my mind, even knowing the consequences which would follow, like the terrible hangover of the day after. I would run to Tesco, take some Gaviscon and a smoothie, and run to work. I felt awful, and no one acknowledged I was ill at work. So that evening routine kept going. I was broken in many different ways, but I simply didn't want to deal with it. I forced myself to be OK with my messy situation, and started to lie about everything. The first lie was when I dropped the hot Irish therapist with the excuse, 'I am doing great, and I will soon move back to my parents, who will help me through the process. Thank you for everything.' It wasn't true. I wasn't going to my parents, but I felt there was no point having a therapist. I wasn't listening to him anymore. In the meantime, I invented thousands of dramatic lies so I wouldn't have to deal with people, work and social gatherings. I seemed to have all the sickness and misfortune in the world, but it wasn't like that, I just wanted to be alone with my drugs and alcohol. Plus, I loved the way people felt sorry for me. I needed mercy.

If I think about it, I was a great liar as a kid, something I believe I was born with, or simply a way to cope with my mother being constantly mean and judgmental towards me. I had such a great imagination that people really believed the stories I told them. I was really curious about everything also, because I didn't have a lot of input from my mother or family. Once, I made a cousin believe that I could read, even though I couldn't. I was four, and took a book and started to follow the sentences, inventing a story out of nowhere. After half an hour, my cousin realised I wasn't reading, and that I was not able to read. She was so surprised because I had acted it perfectly: it was this same perfection that I used when telling lies.

The situation was getting out of control. People started to realise that something was wrong with me, but when they questioned me, I would just make a smiley face saying they were wrong, and that everything was fine. Then June arrived, the weather was mild, and everyone was ready to be part of the great Olympics event. At work, my colleague

Samantha was going to get married soon, and Tara, the colleague that I shared a desk with, called me to the staff room and said:

'Daniel, we are preparing a surprise bachelorette party for Samantha, and we want you to be there, so please make sure you don't have any plans, because we will get crazy. If you don't come, she will be offended, plus, listen to this: we are going to Field Day for free.' She was so excited about it that I had to act as excited as well. I didn't want to go, but I couldn't dream up a lie at that moment. I could say that my dog died, but this was an excuse I had used too many times. As much as I didn't want to deal with this situation and would rather cheat my way through the weekend with wine and pills, I forced myself to go, even if the idea of a festival full of people, loud music and drunk, high folks made me really anxious.

The day came, and I was there in front of the entrance with my medicines hidden inside the sole of my shoes. It was something a friend had taught me, to open slightly the sole of a Vans sneaker, and place the drugs in there.

That year there were many cool artists in the line-up: Metronomy, When Saints Go Machine, Grimes, Blood Orange and many others. Victoria Park became a giant theme park: people with flowers in their hair, games and little markets, people sitting in the grass talking, bottles of alcohol everywhere and the sky saying to all of us, 'it's going to rain.'

We were a group of 10 or more, wearing a horrible T-shirts with 'Team Bride' written in capital letters. The bride-to-be, Samantha, had a long rose dress and a tiara made of tiny cocks: such a cliché, but she loved it. We were as loud as ever, and I was slightly drunk, because we had already had two pints before entering the festival. We were screaming and laughing and taking pictures with our blackberries and iPhones.

'Time to drink!' screamed Tara, taking out an enormous bottle of vodka from her bra. She was a wild party girl and knew how to hide alcohol, taking it out during any event, or in clubs.

My mind pumped that moment. A voice screamed out loud in my head, 'Daniel, drink time, go to take your pills.' The voices in my head were a kind of best friend at that time. I slowly learned not to talk to myself, and just to keep the conversation going for hours in my head. I was mad, but totally OK with it, so I went to the toilet, took off my left shoe, opened the sole, took two pills in my hand, and placed them underneath my tongue. Then I went out, grabbed the bottle from Tara's hands, and drank a big sip of vodka.

In an instant, I was drunk, high, and dizzy. I felt amazing, so I went to Samantha and said, 'Darling, you will be the most beautiful bride in the world. I am so happy and proud of you.' She hugged me, clearly drunk too, and said something like, 'I love you, Daniel, even if you are the worst liar in the world!' I didn't care, I was fine with who I was.

Music started, the festival was on, and everyone ran to the stage, while I stayed where I was, dancing to Blood Orange. The first song was 'Champagne Coast.'

I was so high that I just allowed my body to move, following the beat while the lyrics went on and on. 'Come into my bedroom, come into my bedroom, come into my bedroom.' My body was moving as if I was floating in the air. My hips went left to right and my arms up in the air. I felt sexy and powerful as ever. I was free and strangely grounded. Many people were looking at me, and joined me in that freedom dance. I felt like the queen of my land with all my subjects around me. And then a guy came towards me and danced with me. He took my hand and let me twirl, I laughed out loud, and he smiled, laughing too, then pressed his body against mine, sensually moving his hips. I moved mine in the same way. I felt the energy crossing our bodies. Everything felt so good and endless. He kissed my neck and I kissed his lips.

'So tell me what the joy of giving is if you're never pleased/ On my last strength against you/Baby, tell me what you need,' he sang in my ears. I felt as if my mind had suddenly gained clarity. I had finally found love in the craziest place ever.

'Hey, I am Simon!' he said at the end of the song, with everyone screaming and clapping out loud to Blood Orange. A mix of feelings started to run through my veins. I felt excited, calm, happy, confused and horny, but most importantly,

I felt loved.

'I'm Daniel, would you like a pint?' Was my only answer. I had felt that we understood each other with one simple look. He nodded, took my hand, and followed me.

We walked in silence towards the bar. Being high, I felt awkward with the situation and didn't know how to start a conversation. I didn't want to say something stupid to someone I felt I had fallen in love with already.

He stopped looking at me and said, 'I am Simon, 19 years old. I am 6'2" and I am from Kent. I live in Shadwell and I study English with Creative Writing at Goldsmiths, and I also work part-time in Urban Outfitters.'

'Oh, that's a lot of information there,' I remember saying in a sarcastic way. He laughed and added, 'Sorry, I'm high, and I can be totally weird'. I was so pleased I was not the only one high, and said, 'No worries, we are both high, and I can be weird also when I am sober, so be prepared for it.' He hugged me and we kissed.

We both drank a Red Stripe beer and sat on the grass. There was this insane sensation in the air. People were all enjoying the moment, and I felt overjoyed by the love I could breathe in all around me, plus, I was so attracted to him that I just wanted to rip off his clothes and have sex with him there and then in front of everyone.

I don't have a standard type of man I like. I mostly get attracted by what I am feeling at that moment, and if the person is curious enough to catch my attention. I love the dark souls who have a strange aura of secrecy.

I am totally out of queers' tribes. I love anyone and everyone at the same time. I am not polyamorous, but I just love the feeling of love, and being loved.

Simon was tall, with dark green eyes, brown wavy messy hair, wearing a Topman printed shirt, a pair of black shorts and black Air Max, a must-have fashion product of that period.

'I usually don't dance with someone out of nowhere, but I felt your energy growing in me and I couldn't not come and dance with you,' he said, while staring at me and touching my hands as if he was afraid to lose me. I felt strangely shy and emotional. I kept nodding and smiling till he asked, 'Would you like a bump? It is meow meow.' He placed a tiny bit of powder on the top of a key, put it under my nose and I snorted, not even realising what I was doing. I was totally into him, and at that moment, he could have raped me and I felt I would be OK with it, because I regarded this as my last opportunity to be loved.

For those that don't know what 'meow meow' is, let me give you a quick explanation. In that period, mephedrone was everywhere, along with MD and coke. A few years ago, you could buy it online, but then it became illegal. It was still very easy to find a dealer that would sell it in a tiny plastic bag with a marijuana leaf stamped on top of it. It cost £20, quite cheap even for those who were broke most of the time. It was a cheaper version of MD, but with a horrible taste and a terrible come down the next day. It was mostly used in the community for sex. It causes all your inhibitions to leave your body. It was a drug everyone wanted and used in that period.

The drug took effect within seconds. It was my first time taking a recreational drug in many years. I'd taken some recreational drugs in my university time (mostly coke) but I stopped quickly because I ended up broke every month, then my ex arrived and snorted everything possible, but because of this I had a terrible problem with addiction as well, which I later understood was part of being bipolar.

At that moment, when the meow meow kicked my body, I felt powerful, amazing, horny, and just wanted to dance and chat.

'Simon, let's dance,' I said, and we stood up and started to move our bodies, letting the musical vibrations touch us all over. We hugged, we kissed, we touched each other's bodies, we fell on the grass and took off our shirts. We didn't care about anything until a guard came and said, 'Hey guys, this is not a sexual party, you need to leave.'

We stood up, confused and a bit ashamed, put our shirts on, and left the festival.

We walked to the other side of Victoria Park, by Mile End. We took more bumps, without caring about the people around us, and started to talk.

'We can go to mine if you want, we can stay there. We can watch a movie or whatever. I am obsessed with Miranda, have you watched it? My God, you are so damn beautiful, tell me more about you. I have this feeling we already met in the past. I can feel you. Let's go to Sainsbury's in front of the station and grab some drinks. Would you like to eat? I am not hungry, but I am OK with grabbing something for later: sorry, sorry, too many things! I am high as hell!' He was terribly talkative, I found it so funny.

I laughed so much and kissed him. In that walk to his house, I shared my whole life story with him in 2 minutes, while he nodded and kept saying, 'You are fantastic!' I'm not sure if he was really listening to all of my dramas, but I felt as if someone was finally listening to me. I wasn't lonely anymore.

We grabbed a few Red Stripes, a Sainsbury's meal deal for later, and went to his house near Bow Church.

He lived in an old Victorian house, with posh furniture and a big window looking out onto the street. The black leather sofa was massive, and he had a big posh wooden table with many papers on top. There was also a big green library with many books. I was mesmerised by the place, and while he opened a can of beer for me, he said, 'I live with a friend who is quite wealthy. We have known each other since we were kids. She is in Berlin for work, she is a managing director for a finance firm. And, happily, she is coming back next month, so we have the house all to ourselves for all the days we will stay together, because I feel I need you in my life right now.' I was shocked by these words, no one had ever said anything like that to me. I had mixed feelings. I was flattered, but also a bit confused. How did he need me that badly?

He took his laptop and put on Rihanna, who sang loudly, 'We found love in a hopeless place,' another line of drugs, and we got naked, kissing each other's bodies, then falling to the floor having the highest sex ever.

We stayed up all night and the day after, chatting, kissing, having sex and eventually eating something. I felt I could live like this forever. I liked him so much, he made me feel appreciated, the only thing I needed at that moment. I felt confident enough to share what had happened to me with my mental health struggle, and he hugged me and said, 'It will all be fine if you stay with me.'

I fell asleep on his chest, but in the middle of the night I woke up with a panic attack, feeling guilt about taking drugs, drinking, and the shock of how I had attempted suicide and how my heart was broken. I couldn't breathe, and I started to cry out loud. He woke up, kissed me and said 'Hey, I am here, it is normal, you are having a come-down. Breathe, everything your mind is saying to you is just a thought, not the reality, be here with me. Everything is fine, everything is fine'.

I was calm, and finally felt clear about the come-down experience. On Monday, I called in sick at work, inventing a stomach bug. We spent all day sober, watching Miranda and EastEnders, eating junk food. He was into me even sober, and that made me feel good, even if I knew in my heart that it was just the beginning of the end.

Various Storms & Saints

London was booming, the Olympics were happening, and we were all waiting for the Spice Girls reunion, which would take place during the opening show. The Daily Mail headlines kept asking, 'Will Posh Spice be there?'

The stage was set for thousands of events around town, and there were so many tourists that the Central Line was always packed to capacity.

Simon and I became a couple: he, a 19-year-old student, and me, a 25-year-old unstable person.

During the first weeks of the relationship, he introduced me to his best friends, including Leila, a Norwegian girl who hated me, because she loved Simon not just as a friend but also as a potential partner. Simon said that during a drug party, they had had sex, and from that moment she was jealous as hell about him. We went to cool parties, taking drugs and drinking alcohol. We were high 4 days a week, and I stopped taking my antidepressants, not even caring to say anything to my GP, who thought that I had moved back to my parents' home. I had love now, and that was what mattered most to me, even if my version of reality was confused and dark.

I was deeply in love with Simon, and he with me, but the

way he showed me love was quite icy. I blamed this upon his being British. He didn't know how to be as passionate as a Latino person like me. We had sex constantly, and it was only at these moments that he would say how much he loved me.

But we got along. He was always next to me during my come-downs and hangovers, and I was constantly there if he needed anything. I couldn't bear the thought of losing him, and I felt that without him, my life would be over.

I was dealing with a strange jealousy as well. I hated when people approached him, even if it was a friend, it would make me feel mad. I didn't want to lose him. I felt he was the love I could live with for the rest of my life.

But something was off in this relationship. Most of the time, I felt insecure about the fact I created dramas out of nowhere from the tiniest of situations. I was constantly afraid he would cheat on me, and that his friends might be talking about me behind my back: something they probably did because, in their eyes, I was completely insane. When he was going out with his friends, I would text him constantly, pretending I was feeling sick, and that I needed him, or that I had lost my keys and needed to go to his place. At the beginning, he would reply, reassuring me, but after a while, he started to ignore my messages. As I understood that I was becoming too much for him, I began to accept and do everything he wanted me to do. I was literally cancelling myself as an individual. I was his shadow, and ceased having a personal life.

Each weekend we would take drugs, and this was starting to have a detrimental effect on the relationship. My hangovers and come-downs were dramatic, and as much as he was there comforting me, I kept spewing out all of my insecurities in front of him. He was clearly not happy, and I was as lost as ever.

I had lost my appetite, and my meals consisted of crisps or water. I was getting skinny and becoming paranoid about my figure. I knew he loved super-skinny guys, and I became one. People around me kept asking if I was OK, remarking that I was too skinny, but I answered that everything was fine, that I had become skinny because I was now a vegan. I was simply eating air and drinking beer.

In late October 2012, I had to travel to Berlin for work. The company I was working for was growing, and they needed someone there to help train the Head Office employees. This meant three weeks out of London in a city I had never been to before, and also, far from Simon. I couldn't cope with the situation, and something in my mind kept telling me, 'this is the end.'

The day of the flight, Simon took me to the airport, kissed me, and said, 'Have a good time, and please also try to enjoy the city. I know it is for work, but you need to chill out. I promise I will come to visit you next weekend.' I felt comforted, even if I was very fearful he would cheat on me during those weeks.

For the entire flight, I was confused. I wasn't ready to live that distance from him, and I cried nervously for the entire journey with big black sunglasses on. I didn't want people to see how messed up I was at that moment. The flight landed, and I turned on my phone ready to call Simon, but a message popped up:

'I am sorry to tell you this via message, but I have decided that it is better we have a break, Simon.'

I almost fainted, and it took me a few minutes to understand where I was, and what I was doing there. As soon as we entered the airport with the bus, I ran to the toilet to puke. My biggest fear had been realised, and I felt as though it would kill me.

The days in Berlin were horrible: my mind was somewhere else. I kept trying to call his phone, but he wouldn't answer. Then I started calling his friends, who simply told me, 'We don't want to be part of your problem.' I wrote to all the people we knew, asking if they had any news of Simon, but I just kept receiving vague answers. It seemed as though the whole of London knew something and didn't want to tell me.

I couldn't eat or sleep. I spent every evening crying. And work was not going well: all of my training was messy, and people were shocked by how horrible I looked, with my eyes constantly red, and my hands shaking.

The three weeks seemed endless, and finally the day arrived when I could return to London. My director told me to take a few days off as soon as I explained what had happened. I apologised for all the mess I had created in Berlin. She wasn't happy, because the feedback had been horrible, but she gave me a hug, assuring me that everything would be fine.

I kept going to knock on the door of Simon's house, but no one would answer. He had simply vanished, leaving my heart in pieces. Every day, I went to the university, to cafés and clubs he used to frequent, but I could find no trace of him. No one knew where he was.

I didn't know what to do. I was alone, and dying inside.

Then the weekend came. I just wanted to get smashed and maybe die during it. I couldn't cope with that silence.

I called the dealer who came to my house to deliver what I needed, and I ended up spending £200 on drugs. He was the same one that used to sell to Simon and apparently, he had vanished from him also.

I dressed up, snorted a few lines, jumped in an Uber and went to The Joiners' Arms in Hackney Road. At that time, it was the best place to hang out in East London, along with East Bloc and the George and Dragon.

The guard at the entrance knew me, so he let me inside, and many people got angry as I skipped the long queue.

Inside, it was packed. The music was loud, and I was high. I ordered a pint and went in search of Simon.

The club was small, with leather sofas on the opposite side of the bar, and, closer to it, the DJ playing music. To go to the smoking area, you had to pass through a thick clear plastic curtain door. The bathroom was the only well-lit part of the club, with silver metal cubicles and a terrible smell of meph and piss. Everyone in East London loved to go here, it was the coolest place with East Londoners, artsy people, many of them high or drunk.

Simon wasn't there. I couldn't handle the situation, went to the loo, took my key, dove it in my bag of meph, and snorted loudly, just as everyone in the adjacent cubicles were doing.

I was so numb and high that I forgot what had happened, starting to dance crazily. Dancing and drugs were my only way to escape from my mind at that moment. I was sweaty and messy, but I felt so beautiful and good that I couldn't believe how someone could leave me in that way. I was broken and crazy.

After a while, I moved to the smoking area, and sat by the white wall with people everywhere smoking, laughing and screaming. I kept staring at the tableau, I could see just mouths moving and distorted faces all around me.

'Hey Daniel, hey, are you OK? Where is Simon?' I lifted my head to find Thomas, one of Simon's friends. My face was shocked, because I didn't understand why he was asking me about Simon. Didn't he know what had happened?

'Uhm, hey, yeah I am fine, you? Simon...' I laughed. 'He broke up with me via message and disappeared out of my life. Might you know where he is, by any chance?' I said, shaking, waiting to receive, finally, the answer I needed to hear.

Thomas sat down and hugged me, 'I am sorry Daniel, I didn't know. He went to Kent weeks ago, but I thought he was back. Hey, how are you feeling?'

I was so devastated, frustrated and sad that tears ran down my face, 'Well, I don't feel well. I am trying my best, but it is hard.' He hugged me again and said, 'Yeah, you know since the beginning, I said to him to not play that game with you.' I glanced at him. My heart stopped. 'Which game?' I asked.

'Fuck! I shouldn't have said anything, I'm sorry. Listen, I don't want to have problems, forget what I said.'

I stopped him from standing up and walking away, took his hand, and said, 'Just tell me, or I will ruin your night.' I felt a terrible anger in me as the devil took my body. His face changed, and he sat back, afraid of my words. I was high enough to create the biggest drama on earth there.

'OK, listen, I never told you anything, OK? So please don't put me in the middle. Simon stayed with you because he wanted to make Jacob jealous. Jacob was his ex-boyfriend, and Simon wanted revenge, for whatever reason, so at the beginning, he pretended to be with you. Then he got attached to you, but his mind was always on Jacob and how to get him back. I told him not to play this game, or someone would burn, and I am sorry if you are the one burned, because you don't deserve it.'

I couldn't speak, I was shocked. For almost six months I believed I was loved, but instead, it was all fake. How could I not have seen that? I felt so stupid.

Tears started to pour down my face, and Thomas hugged me, whispering in my ear, 'Daniel, everything is fine. Don't get upset, I am here, let's go out.'

'I love him, and I feel I can't cope with all that, I am dying inside. Why do something like that with me, how did he know I had something with Jacob? How would Jacob care about it?' I started crying, and Thomas placed his hands around my face and stared at me and said, 'You are not alone, and you can cope with this, I am here, let's go out and have a walk, you can't stay here in this state, let's go.'

We left the club. It was a cold evening. I was wearing my creepers, shorts and an oversize sheepskin coat, and Thomas, a Misfit sweatshirt and a padded jeans jacket. We walked down Hackney Road. He kept placing his arms around me, checking I was OK. We turned left, passing through Hackney Farm, taking the road that took us to Broadway Market. We sat on a bench. It was early morning, and outside the pubs, people were smoking. London was always on fire, and here I was, burning up in it.

I took my bag of drugs and my keys and passed them to Thomas, who snorted a bit, then passed it back to me. I did the same.

'Daniel, I am sorry. I know that this is not the right moment, but when I say I am always here for you, it is because I really fancy you, and I would never do what Simon did to you. I am ready to stop my friendship with Simon just to stay with you.' Too many things were happening at the same moment. I was coming to terms with the truth about why Simon left me, and at the same time Thomas was telling me he liked me. I was high. I stared at him, smiled, and kissed his lips.

We were two lost souls looking for the same thing: to be loved.

Days passed, and Thomas and I were still together. Such a charming guy from East London, I felt he was falling in love with me. This was something I enjoyed, but I did not feel anything for him. I just wanted someone next to me. I couldn't cope with life without someone by my side.

I couldn't stand to be lonely, so I was keen to stay with anyone, even someone for whom I had no feelings.

Drugs and alcohol were my priority. I was sober just two days a week, and those two days seemed a hell to me. Work was not going well: I was constantly calling in sick, and as much as I had great support from my colleagues and director, I didn't want to be part of any of it. My priority was to get high and drunk.

My mood swings were horrible. In the same ten minutes, I could be happy, sad, hyperactive, angry, and many other things. Suicidal thoughts came back to haunt me, and I spent many nights imagining how my funeral would be. I wondered whether Simon, Jacob or Thomas would cry or say anything. My birthday passed, with me high, not noticing how many people sent messages or called me. In the blink of an eye Christmas was upon us. Thomas invited me to his family house. I said no, as I was too embarrassed to go there. I was afraid I would cause a scene, getting high between meals and gift exchanges.

He understood, and I spent Christmas Day snorting lines of meph with a glass of wine. I had to endure the classic Christmas call to my parents, during which they would make me feel guilty that I wasn't there to celebrate with them.

'Hey mum, Merry Christmas! Yes, yes, maybe next year. Love you all.' I ended the call so I wouldn't have to listen to my mother playing the victim with me.

I was so high and bored that the only thing I could think of doing was to download the Grindr app and find someone to share that moment with me. I didn't care about Thomas at all, I just wanted to have my fun.

That evening, I learned I just wanted to be in bed with different people as hopeless as me, getting high and having sex. I was not myself anymore.

I could hear a voice in my head telling me:

'You are doing great right now: have your fun and die.'

My Boy Builds Coffins

And Thomas became John, John became Terry, Terry became Alberto. Alberto became Shane, Shane became Robbie, and Robbie became another 100 names I don't even remember anymore. Most of the time I was high, having fun with many men from all over the world that I would invite to my house for a chem party.

Every Saturday night, I would go to XXL club in Vauxhall, the gay bear heaven of London. The club was giant, with enormous spaces for dancing to different types of music, a seating area with sofas, and a dark room. Whilst in there, I would keep changing dancing rooms, in the meantime going to the bathroom to take a line of drugs, then running to the dark room to get fucked, and in the end going back to dance for a bit, even if, in that high state, I didn't have much rhythm in me. I would end by taking someone home to spend the night with. All strangers, high and horny as me. The day or two after would be all about hangovers and living through terrible come-downs, so terrible that I would lie on the floor of my room and cry for hours. In those moments, my mind screamed out loud for help, but I didn't want to hear it. I was afraid to ask for support and I felt that God was judging me, and that was painful enough. Once, I tried to call my mother to ask for help, but she answered by saying: "Listen son, I have your aunties here, I will call you later," and that never happened. I was alone with my drugs.

At the time, I weighed 11 stone, something quite sick for someone 6'3" tall like me. I was just skin and bone, and my skin looked pale and sweaty all the time.

Most nights, I would stay in front of the mirror, contemplating my bones, and counting all my ribs. In my eyes, I loved being skinny, but I also felt I was dying inside, breathing through paranoia and fear.

During one of the nights in XXL, I met Farez, a Lebanese guy. The way we met was quite funny: we were in the queue to go to the bathroom, and he grabbed my hand and said, 'Mate, your nose is bleached white, it seems you fell into a bag of meph. Come here, let me clean…' and he passed his fingers around my nose, then licked them and said, 'Oh, good quality. Who is your dealer?' I remember being slightly in shock, laughing so loud that I almost peed myself. From that moment, we became firm friends, and in time we became best friends. Farez's family came to London in the 1960s to make their fortune. This happened for real when his father opened a fabric wholesale store in East London. Farez left home at the age of 17, he didn't want to go to university and study, his dream was simply to become famous. He didn't have any particular talent, but he had the kind of looks and charismatic approach to life which everyone he met found mesmerising. He worked for a retail store in Oxford Street. He didn't care much about it, calling in sick every other day. He lived mostly in the same way as I did, drugs were his only way to cope with life. He was high almost seven days a week, but no one could really see it. He was always composed and clean. We had many things in common, such as toxic relationships, manipulative mothers and mental health issues which had never really been dealt with. We had the same taste in men and music. From Thursday onwards he would spend the weekend at my place. We had lines of meph and ketamine on an Ikea white plate, drinking cheap cider from Tesco, and talking about a multitude of things. Sometimes we went really deep in conversation, all about the way we perceived life at that moment, and how we imagined our futures might be.

'You know Daniel, I am a drug addict, and I think everyone can see that. I am aware of it. I am happy about that. I don't care what people see and think about me, because I choose to be addicted, and I will be that for the rest of my days.' He looked at me while cutting the next lines of meph, 'I said to my manager at work and all my colleagues that I am an addict and that's why I will always call in sick. They tried to give support, but I don't care, the only support I need is *this*... (he stopped to snort it.) I love drugs. I prefer to be high than to deal with a life in which people don't see me. I was invisible to my family, to my lovers and many friends: I can't be that shit anymore. I want to be famous in East London, I want to be recognized in the street as the hot fashion Lebanese drug addict...' we looked at each other, sharing the greatest laughter of all.

I felt the same, even if I didn't regard myself as a drug addict, but rather as someone who had lost the plot of his life and found that drugs were the only way to give himself the power to do anything. My world was dark, but I had flashes of light every once in a while.

At work, I was simply a mess. I was capable of going to work high, which made me terribly efficient, but as soon as the drug effects wore off, the come-down was terrible. I would fake sickness in order to leave early. In 2013, everyone was high, and most of my colleagues were in the same boat. We were all looking for an escape from that hectic life.

As no one took too much notice, I also started to make up lies, for example, my father dying, my mother getting sick, or my sister having a car accident, or that I had to return to visit them. So no one seemed to notice the progression of my addiction, even if many stopped talking to me from one day to the next. It was a similar situation in my personal life. My lies were getting bigger and bigger, to the point where everything became messy and unreal, and people stopped believing in me.

In East London, I would often go clubbing to Dalston Superstore or East Bloc. Farez and I started to be recognisable in the club scene. We met a lot of people, and gravitated towards those who had similar drug issues. We were the new club kids of East London, going to parties and wearing crazy clothes just to get the attention of everyone around us.

Farez was with me almost every day, and ended up moving into my room, which my flatmates weren't too happy about. I didn't care much, as the rental contract was under my name, and my landlord simply wanted someone who would pay the rent each month. Every time I had someone to take home, Farez would leave the house, and vice versa. We promised to never ruin our friendship by having sex together: a wise decision. We slept in the same bed, and each night we hugged each other. He was the only one who understood me, and I was the only one who understood him.

Our support for each other was something beyond special. He was always there for me during my hangovers and comedowns, giving me the calmness and love I needed. We used to cry together, creating future plans on pieces of paper that we attached to the wall of my room. This was our way to escape for a few moments the sadness we lived with.

Once a week we would go to the gay saunas in Limehouse or Vauxhall. Most of the time, this was simply to enjoy the sauna itself, and other times because we were horny as hell.

We would go there together, walking through all the labyrinths, rooms, saunas and jacuzzis, taking lines of meph and drinking GHB. We met many people there who were as high as we were. And as soon as we found someone to spend time with, we would say goodbye, promising to search for each other afterwards, screaming our names out loud through that darkness of a place.

That place was a kind of hell on earth: you could find whatever you wanted, from the young guy on his first experience, to the perverted men that would not leave you until you gave them something. You could be raped there, but, being in that state, you couldn't understand if it was consensual or just part of your imagination.

It was a funny thing to have saunas or jacuzzis where hundreds of men would be having sex in the cabins around the establishment.

We used to spend the entire evening and night there, leaving at around 7 a.m., go to work, or sleep at mine.

Lana Del Rey became our muse for that entire time, 'we are born to die in this summertime sadness,' we used to say to each other. In 2013, she came out with 'Tropico,' a movie with all her songs, and that became our anthem. We wanted to be fucking crazy all the time, and we went to pole dance classes for a few weeks before both of us quit. If you have never watched 'Tropico,' I suggest you watch it: it is both an amazing representation of her songs, and also of the way we lived at that time.

Another year passed, and I was skinny, depressed and scared of life. I changed partners every three days, and was constantly visiting the sexual health clinic. That became my Monday appointment; having jabs for different STDs, and worrying about whether I was HIV positive.

Whitechapel health clinic became our second home, and Farez and I would go together, squeezing each other's hands in the waiting room saying, 'if we are positive, we have to take care of each other.' We were completely delusional.

He was the brother I had never had: there was never any judgement between us, only honesty and care. Though most people thought we were a couple, we loved each other in a brotherly way, cheering each other every time something was breaking the other's heart or mind.

Then, tragedy struck. On New Year's Eve, we were invited to a house party. We brought all the drugs we wanted, and prepared to start the New Year high. Unconsciously, we were a bad influence on each other. In the back of our minds, we wanted sobriety, but that was too difficult to attain.

The house party was in Seven Sisters, at a warehouse which now houses many London artists. The guy that invited us was a painter we had met during our nights at the sauna in Limehouse. He had fallen in love with Farez, and wanted to kiss him at midnight as good luck. What a crazy idea.

When we arrived, the room was packed. Everyone was dancing and having fun. My first thought was: how in the hell could someone live in a place like this? It was a giant industrial loft with dark floors, an open bathroom with just a tiny wall to cover the toilet, and the kitchen in the middle of the room. There was a bar by the entrance and a bathtub in front of the bed that was covered with people sitting and drinking. There was this mixed smell of sweat and lavender air freshener, and the floor was sticky, as if everyone had thrown glue on the floor instead of drinks.

'Latch' by Disclosure was playing loudly. Farez went to say hi to the painter, who pushed him into the corner, kissing him wildly, while I kept on dancing. 'I feel we're close enough. I wanna lock in your love. I think we're close enough. Could I lock in your love, baby?' sang Sam Smith out loud from the speakers. I could feel the sound kicking my body, and the drugs we took on the cab starting to blur my mind.

'Hey brother, stop dancing like a slut, haha!' Farez said to me, 'Let's go there in the corner, I need to get higher after that awful kiss. Gosh, his tongue was like a food processor, fuck that!'

We moved to one corner of the room, closer to the bed, where Farez introduced me to Carl, Robert and John: three fashion queer people, who were ready to share drugs with us.

We started to chat about everything and nothing at the same time. I don't remember much of that conversation, because after 1 minute, Carl started to kiss me. I played the one in shock, even if I was totally OK with it. He took my hands and said, 'I want to introduce you to my boyfriend: Simon, this is Daniel. I found our threesome!' And that was what shocked me the most.

My heart raced when I saw Simon.

Simon, the man who ghosted me and broke my heart and life last year, taking his leave of me with a simple text message while I was in Berlin.

He glanced up, then said, 'Hey, Daniel, nice to meet you!' As if he had never met me before. I walked away, took Farez, and we went out for a smoke. I was shaking, and I kept walking left and right, bubbling over with emotion.

'Daniel, what happened? Man, what is going on?' Farez asked worriedly, and at that moment, a panic attack ran through my body. I felt like I couldn't breathe anymore. He sat me down and slowly helped me to breathe, saying, 'Brother, everything is fine, I am here with you.' 'Do you remember when I told you about Simon?' I looked at Farez in a startled way.

'Yes, that is Simon, and he also pretended he had never met me, son of a bitch!' I stood up and ran towards the house, but Farez stopped me, took a pill of ecstasy from his bag, and placed it in my mouth saying, 'Hey, I got you. He is clearly a dickhead, but also someone from your past that you don't need anymore. Today is our day, and we have to have fun and not drama. Give me your hand and let's go dance.'

How could I have fun in that situation? I was so confused and didn't understand what to do, or how to behave, until the pill started to work, and I felt as though I was a butterfly flying around the room. In my eyes, that place became a land of trees and birds. I felt I was in a safer place suddenly.

Simon approached me, asking if we could have a chat outside. I nodded and went with him. I was too much in my own world to understand what was going on. I kissed him while he was apologising about the past, and left him there saying, 'It's OK, I wish you were dead, but not today, go and have fun.'

I went back to the dancefloor where Farez was the one dancing as a strip clubber, something I so much loved to see. He had this way of moving his body that hypnotised anyone around him. He looked at me, smiled, and fell on the floor.

It was five minutes before midnight. I took him out and called the ambulance along with the other people who had found him in that situation, and we ran to the hospital.

'I am sorry...' The doctor said in the waiting room of the hospital.

My soul brother died on the 1st of January at 1.30 a.m.

Seven Devils

I was devastated. I couldn't feel anything. Doctors and some police questioned me about what had happened. I was in shock, but I confessed to what we had taken during the party, not realising the gravity of the situation.

I didn't know Farez's parents or family at all, but through a mutual friend, we managed to contact them and deliver the worst news you can ever give a parent. There was a strange silence on the other end of the line. Then a broken voice said, 'OK, we are coming.'

I left before they arrived. I was too ashamed. I didn't want to take responsibility for everything, and I already knew how they would scream at me, asking, 'why did I let their child die in that way?'

Leaving the hospital, I felt lonely. I felt fear course through my veins. I started to shake. I had just lost my best friend, and I didn't know what to do.

The streets of East London were still buzzing, parties were still going on, and many people screamed out loud, 'Happy New Year!' A bunch of youngsters came and hugged me, saying, 'Mate, smile: a new year is here, innit?' leaving me there alone, laughing at the way I reacted. I walked back home feeling dead inside. My whole world was broken: I was nothing anymore.

Eventually, I arrived home and closed the door of my room, where I laid down on the floor. I stayed there for hours, while my phone kept ringing. I just wanted to wake up from this nightmare.

The day of the funeral, the club kids of East London joined me. We all dressed in black and carried white roses: Farez's favourite flowers. I didn't eat much during those days, I mainly dealt with the many messages from people enquiring about what had happened, and asking if I was feeling OK.

I was not OK, but, being a proud person, my answer was always, 'no worries, I am fine, I am a big boy.'

For the last goodbye, I respectfully asked his family to play 'Born to die,' his favourite song. They accepted: the music was on, and his mother came to me and gave me a big hug. She said, 'we don't hate you, Daniel. We knew that something like that might happen, but I don't want the same thing to happen to you, so please go and ask for support. That is what Farez would say to you now.'

I felt emotional, and, although I was crying, I felt I didn't need support, I just needed a break from life. A few weeks later, I was fired from my job, another dramatic situation to add to the chaos of my life at that moment.

I managed to ask for benefit support, which meant dealing with a mountain of paperwork. This at least gave me a little breathing space to address all of my problems, but I was totally lost. I felt the world was against me. I couldn't do anything to change that.

In order to try and forget everything, I went back to the same lifestyle I had lived when Farez was still alive. I took drugs each day, had sex with as many people as I could, didn't eat at all, and got very little sleep. In the midst of these dark moments, I went to visit my parents, who asked me to leave early, advising me, 'Get a better life, or you will die the same way as your friend.' Many friends offered support, but I felt I could not accept it, as I was still trying to understand what was happening to me.

Each Saturday morning, I went to Farez's grave in Manor Park. I sat by the grave taking a line of meph, talking to him out loud, and expecting to receive an answer.

During that period, mental health was being given huge coverage on the news and on many social media platforms. For this reason, people around me suggested asking for bereavement support or grief counselling.

Once again, I felt I didn't need support. I just needed a break from my life.

I decided that maybe I needed to go somewhere else, far from London, so I took a train to Edinburgh for a few days, crashing on an old friend's sofa. Even if I felt good being far from London, I felt lost as I was not getting high. After a few days, I returned to London with a voice in my mind saying, 'you needed a break from life.'

Summer came, and I started to feel better, even if my addiction was getting worse. I wrote a contract with myself in my journal, stating that I would get smashed from Friday evening till Sunday morning. Somehow, I felt that this gave me control over my life: I was holding the reins, and happy to keep distorting my reality in this way.

In July 2014, the Lovebox Festival was held in Victoria Park, with an incredible line-up including M.I.A. Her album, 'Matangi' was on my headphones daily, and the hit 'Bad Girls' was playing everywhere.

The club kids and I managed to get hold of free tickets for the festival, thanks to one of them having a friend who worked for one of the sponsors.

We hid drugs everywhere, so we would not be caught at the entrance. We all had sunglasses on, and were dressed in black with tiny shorts, long printed shirts and Dr Martens.

M.I.A.'s performance was interrupted because of sound problems, and after around thirty minutes she left the stage, leaving everyone angry and frustrated.

We all left the festival and went to Dalston Superstore. The bouncer let us jump the queue, causing those waiting in line to get angry, but we were the cool kids of East London, so we didn't care.

We danced, took any drugs available, and I started to make out with almost everyone. After a while, I got bored with this behaviour, and the people around me. I left the party and walked back home through King's High Street, encountering many people who were drunk, high and lost, just like me.

That evening, I had flashbacks of Farez and our great moments together. I felt he was there with me: perhaps because I was high, or simply because I missed my friend so much.

The sky was pitch dark that night. You can't see many stars in London because of the light pollution, but in Shoreditch High Street I could see something bright in all that pitch darkness: a star, perhaps, or maybe a sign, saying, 'it is your time to go.'

When I arrived home, my flatmates weren't there. We didn't have a good relationship anyway. I kept changing flatmates, I was picky in my choice of who could stay around me, plus the lease was in my name, so I was the one deciding everything: this was the only place I could be the queen in my life.

In my messy room, next to the window, there were empty bottles of cider, Farez's ashtray, a small mirror that we used to take lines of drugs, and an 'oyster' travelcard to divide those lines into new realities and visions.

I took my headphones and put on Temple's album, 'Sun Structure.' The first song of the album is 'Shelter Song,' which has an early 70's vibe. It was my time to dance, so I stood up and started to move my body, and the song went, 'So then you keep turning/And you keep turning around/ Keep turning till it all spins off somehow/Dizzy headed banshee of a phosphine capacity.'

My body moved, jumping, helping me to be free and turning all those images to reality. I felt I needed to connect with my brother at that moment, so I took the pack of chems from my pocket and threw them on top of the mirror, then opened the box that was hidden under my bed with all the antidepressants and other medication, put them all on that mirror, and started to crush and mix them all. I took a piece of paper on which I wrote, 'Let my parents know I really loved them,' and left it outside my door. I turned the volume up, rolled a five-pound note, and snorted the biggest line I've ever done. I then passed my finger over the residue, and placed it in my mouth.

That was the end. We really met that night, brother, didn't we?

Light of Love

It is funny how many people describe their walk to death as light at the end of the tunnel, with a voice, or angel, saying, 'It's not your time! Now go back.'

Nothing like that happened to me, but yes, I woke up with a drip in my arm, and many wires attached to my chest, my heart still beating.

I felt lost, not having a clue what had happened. The only glimpse of memory I had was of me dancing, high, in my room, probably the night before.

'Hello Mr Perez, everything is fine. You are in the Royal Hospital of London. Today is the 27th of July, and you slept for a few days. The doctor will come in a second. We are glad you are back,' a tall blonde nurse said, while checking all the machines around me. She had a comforting smile and that creeped me out.

'Miss, I need to go home, I don't know what has happened, but I feel OK, I need to go home!' I said, realising I had done it again: I had attempted suicide again.

And the nurse smiled, rearranging my bedsheets, and saying, 'You will go home after the doctor comes to visit you, OK? For the moment, stay cosy and calm. Everything is fine, and you don't have anything to be afraid of.'

But I was afraid. My heart started to beat faster than ever. I knew I was in trouble, and that I had to go on the same journey I had done in the past, but I was tired of dealing with myself.

'Mr Perez, I am Doctor Knightly. I am happy to see you are awake. How are you feeling?' said the bearded doctor, looking at me and writing something on the record.

'Doctor, I am fine, I need to go home. I can't stay here; I have things to do,' my voice was trembling.

The doctor came closer, smiled at me, checked the drip levels, and said:

'Mr Perez, you are here because you took an overdose. Your heart stopped for a few seconds, but we managed to bring you back. You were in a coma for six days, and you can't leave the hospital at the moment: we have to keep an eye on you. Your flatmates brought you here, and they will be here soon: you are a lucky guy. Now rest, and we will take care of you.'

As soon as he left the room, I started to think about thousands of ways to escape from that situation, but at the same time, another thought struck me: What would I say to people who knew me? What would I say to my family, who hadn't had news of me for days? Those questions kept repeating in my mind, and only one answer came: 'You need to be honest and ask for help.'

My flatmate Roo came after a few hours with a bouquet of daffodils bought in Tesco, probably. He hugged me, the most intense and true hug I had ever received in my life.

'Silly man, you scared us to death: promise you will never do that again! I was sleeping, but when you came back home I heard a big 'bam!' sound coming from your room. I woke up thinking it was a thief or something. Then I saw the note you left by your door. I opened the door and there you were on the floor. I ran and called our neighbour, and we put you under the shower, but you were unconscious, and you started to become white and then blue. So we called an ambulance and, thank God, it came in a few minutes. Sorry to tell you all this, but you scared the life out of me. I am happy you are finally back with us. Listen mate, I think they will ask for a lot of tests, and you will stay here for a few weeks. Just let me know what you need from home and I will pick it up for you.' My heart was in pieces listening to this, and, as much as I wanted to cry out loud, I felt I couldn't, so instead I said:

'Roo, can you lend me your phone? I need to call my family.' He nodded and gave me the phone, and after the first ring, an angry voice answered and screamed:

'What happened? We booked flights to London, but we couldn't find you. We called your friends, but no-one knew anything. You are a stupid kid, always thinking only of yourself and not us. Now that we know you are alive, we won't come. I don't want to waste my time with someone that doesn't care about his family.' and the line went dead, leaving me there in silence, thinking that I needed to wake up to life.

The weeks passed. I left the hospital and went back home. Each day, Roo spent at least 2 hours with me and he was the one who took me to all my appointments with psychologists, therapists, and to NA meetings.

In the Narcotics Anonymous meetings, I always stayed silent, listening to others' stories until the day I had the courage to speak up and tell my story. I thought no one would understand me when I started saying, 'I think I was fucked up since the day I was born,' but, surprisingly, at the end of my talk, people came to hug me, saying how much they resonated with me and my story. I felt I was no longer alone.

The days passed. I stopped clubbing, drinking, and intoxicating myself with drugs and people. I ended my friendship with the club kids of East London, who didn't care much about me not going out with them, or how I was coping with life.

I began to change my life and routine. I needed to leave that darkness that wasn't for me anymore. I started going to cafes and museums, joining writing workshops, meeting new people and openly sharing my life experience.

Roo and I became close friends, and each Thursday evening we went to Cineworld in Canary Wharf to watch a movie. Afterwards, we would sit outside The Ledger Building pub to drink tea and share our personal review of the movie, but also to talk about all aspects of life, about sobriety and how difficult it sometimes was to deal with all the temptation and situations I faced each day in London. As much as I felt strong in my journey of sobriety and healing, I had moments of temptation that I stopped by imagining myself in hospital once again.

Roo suggested I should go for a weekend in the countryside, something I couldn't do because of the low income I had from being on benefits. Money became a big problem, and eventually I found a part-time job at a vintage store on Brick Lane. This helped me, not just economically, but also mentally. I was around cool people from different backgrounds with big dreams: most of them were studying, or trying to find a place in showbusiness. We had a motivational game we did each morning before starting our shift. We would take a piece of paper and write our daily plan to achieve our dreams, giving each other suggestions and advice on how to turn that dream into reality.

After work, we would go to the pub closest to the store, where I would drink a glass of cola zero and talk about all the funny things that had happened with customers.

Each Sunday morning we went for yoga and meditation at a little place in Hackney Wick with the people I had met in NA meetings. Afterwards, we would have tea or coffee in a tiny cafe by the canal. All those little details I was adding to my life became very special and important to me.

Everything was getting better. My life was not a mess at all, and people around me could see a new Daniel they had never seen before.

It was strange to think that a few months before, I had been trapped in a living nightmare, tearing my life apart.

I stopped any kind of dates and sexual intercourse. I had to find myself first. I felt as if I had lost touch with myself many years ago, and that this was *my* time to reconnect and discover the true me.

My family didn't know much. I called them each week, but on the other side of the line there was always anger and frustration in listening to my voice. There wasn't much support, only judgement. My mother was all about 'me, me, me' in our phone calls, to the point that she stopped asking me how I was feeling. Sometimes, the only thing I said via the phone was 'Hello,' and the entire call was just about her. I suffered because of that behaviour. In fact, in my therapy sessions, we went through my past and my family. It was hard for me, because the only memories I had were of a mother who was too controlling and strict: a toxic narcissist and a manipulator. My stepfather didn't have much power in the relationship, and my sister had been suffering from depression since the age of 14, with my mother covering it all up. She didn't want to have something like that in her family, so instead she sent Paloma to Catholic boarding school, thinking that would toughen her up.

In her eyes, I was the rebel, the son who had many problems to deal with. 'It is good you are out in the world because I can't stand you!' she said every time we sat down for a simple conversation.

As the days passed, I began to feel better and better. I kept going to NA meetings, even if I felt that I no longer needed to: Roo and my therapist kept pushing me on that journey. I was three months sober now, and I was mesmerised by how my life was completely clear and beautiful.

Life was treating me right, or maybe I was treating life with an open heart, rather than as an open wound.

I went to Farez's grave many times, to talk to him and let him know about my journey in sobriety. I cried every time. He left us without ever realising he could heal himself by giving up drugs. I also visited his family many times: they took me under their wing. I became their son. His mother would prepare a Tupperware of food to take home. Sometimes we would cry together and then laugh, making jokes about Farez's many strange quirks and idiosyncracies.

I started journaling, writing down my feelings. At first, that felt weird, then it became something I couldn't live without. I never realised the importance of listening and respecting the person I was. And that gave me so much power. I was learning to be OK with the word 'loneliness.'

In October 2014, I took a Megabus to Glasgow, and then a train to Fort William. I needed a quiet place to stay for a few days. Nature was very healing for me, and I wanted to stay in a place far from the cement and chaos that was London.

In Fort William, I went hiking, taking pictures and writing about myself and my environment. Everything was magical: nature was transforming the scene to the brown colours of autumn, one of my favourite seasons. The weather was crisp and chilly, and the smell of wet soil and wood made me fall in love with my surroundings.

On one of those lonely walks, I met an Australian guy called Gabriel.

His plan was to stay for 2 days in Fort William, then go on to Oban. He loved Scotland so much because his grandad was from the Shetlands. Until that moment, I believed I was the only queer going for walks in nature and not talking about fashion or clubbing, but he was like me: just looking for peace and quiet, and the realisation of self-love and self-respect.

We bonded, and spent the entire day together, going to have dinner at the Garrison West pub bistro where we had fish and chips, the best you could find in town. We exchanged phone numbers, and the morning after he sent me a message saying he had changed his plan. He would stay a little longer in Fort William. He was surprised to have found a person like me, and he wanted us to spend more time together.

I liked Gabriel, but at the same time, I didn't want to be involved in anything. I wasn't ready to deal with someone else's emotions. But in my heart, I heard a voice saying, 'just let go of all your fears, and enjoy the situation as it is, without judgement and paranoia.'

We went for long walks, where he would take my hand and smile at me. It was a sweet thing to do, and I felt totally OK with it. We began to be open with one another, and we shared our life experiences. I talked about Farez, the messy life I had had before, my NA meetings, and the fact I would soon be three-and-a-half months sober. I felt it was easy to be open with my feelings to him: I didn't feel judged at all, and at the same time, I thought how much I had matured as a person to be able to open up in that way. During my talk, he would nod, smile, and say things such as, 'you are a great guy: I am sure Farez is proud of you, wherever he is.' This made me feel good about the way I was dealing with myself.

He told me about his last relationship, and how a heartbreak had become a long depression. He had left Melbourne to find himself in the world outside. He had felt oppressed for most of his life, and his coming out as a gay man had not been accepted by his family, who were angry with him. He talked about all the times his mother had taken him to the doctors to try and get rid of the homosexuality, which, in her eyes, was like a terrible sickness.

One morning, we prepared ourselves to climb Ben Nevis. We met at 9am at The Wild Cat, a cosy, beautiful cafe in the High Street of Fort William. I was waiting for Gabriel, reading all the bad reviews about Lindsay Lohan's debut in the West End with Speed-the-Plow. My friends in London were posting about it everywhere; it was all about how the play was amazing because Lindsay Lohan was in it. We all loved her in Mean Girls: that is such an iconic movie, and I think we queer guys loved Lindsay no matter what.

Gabriel arrived, this tall, blonde guy with black eyes, a tiny bit shorter than me, with a beautiful, sweet smile:

'Hey beautiful.' He said, 'Let's go, are you ready?' I nodded, took my bag, and gave him a hug.

Ben Nevis was a big, challenging journey because of the difficulty in getting to the summit, which is almost always in cloud, and can be dangerous. But that morning was different. We could see all the way to the summit, and the challenging walk which awaited us.

The walk was tough, but the scenery was spectacular. Everything was green, with beautiful details and landscapes. The healing power of Mother Nature was in evidence everywhere.

'Daniel, I have to ask you something. It might sound a bit

weird. I really like you, and I was wondering if you would like to travel the world with me?' Gabriel asked, looking at me, and hoping to hear an instant 'yes.' But as much as I was feeling flattered by the request and the fact that he liked me, I was on my own journey of self-discovery. I liked him very much, but it was my time to discover myself and not share my world with anyone else. I was finally listening to myself, and I didn't want to repeat the same old pattern. I didn't need someone to confirm that I was OK alone. 'Gabriel, as much as I like you and the idea of travelling the world, I can't right now. I am on this journey of self-discovery, and I need to learn to stand on my own feet.'

I could see the sadness in his eyes, so I took his hand and kissed him. I could feel his heartbeat while our lips were touching: he placed his arms around me, and my heart felt light and warm.

I didn't kiss him to make him happy, this kiss was different, and it is hard to explain it.

We smiled at each other, and hand in hand, we continued our walk to the summit. The weather kept changing, and unfortunately we didn't make it to the top: it was too dangerous, so we stopped, sat down and ate our £3 meal deal from Tesco, enjoying the view in front of us.

I felt confident at that moment, and ready to listen to someone else. Active listening was never something I had been good at, but in going to NA meetings I had learnt the importance of listening to others. Gabriel and I could talk for hours about everything. We were open to each other, and we shared our life stories.

For the next two days, Gabriel stayed in my hotel room. The weather was not the best for having outdoor adventures, so we decided we needed that cosy time together: using room service, watching movies, reading books and eventually having sex. We cuddled naked after sex, enjoying the touch of our bodies under the duvet. He would place his hand on my heart and count the beats, saying things such as, 'That beat is mine, and this one is ours,' or, 'I want this time to be endless.' We would dream about having babies, and what features the baby would have.

'The colour of my eyes would be yours, and the shape, mine.' I would say to him. 'The smiles will be yours, but with my hair.' All these crazy conversations that I knew would end in a few days. As much as one part of me wanted to live like that forever, the other part kept sending me an alert message, 'you need to focus on *you*.'

We had the idea of writing a page in each other's journal to remind us of these magical moments together.

He wrote a full five pages about all the feelings he had for me, and how he was sure he had found the love of his life. I wrote three pages describing that what we were living was Eden, and we should not be tempted into emotional sin: we needed to be realistic about the situation, and I didn't want to give false promises. I had lived most of my life trying to find a person who would heal my mind, but at that moment, I didn't need this anymore. I could heal myself alone, and even if the temptation of falling into the old mistakes again was something real, I couldn't, and I felt strong in my decision.

The day of the departure, my heart contracted at the idea of being alone again. I cried a couple of times alone in the bathroom while getting ready. For a moment I felt hopeless, but I remembered what my therapist had once told me: 'Accept all of the emotions openly, and never try to conceal them.' And that helped me to really understand the importance of self-listening.

The time came to say goodbye. He cried at the station, I cried on the train, and we promised to keep in touch and see each other again soon.

'I know we spent only a short period of time together, but I think I love you,' he said, with tearful eyes. I hugged him in silence: we said goodbye, and I jumped on my train to Glasgow before boarding the Megabus to London.

After a while, I received a picture of the two of us on my phone with the caption, 'I miss you badly.' I left it there for a few hours before answering, 'me too.'

For the first time in a long time, I felt OK with what was happening. I was not getting dramatic and crazy about the situation. I could have stayed there with Gabriel and travelled around the world, but it wasn't the right time. I was not ready to give up my freedom for anyone at that moment. We think we need someone to grow old with, but this is just an idea imposed upon us by society.

Solitude is not a bad thing; it is a great way to learn about who you truly are.

Back in London, I decided it was my time to build a new life, starting from changing my home, my behaviour toward myself and my routine. As much as I loved my room, I still had many memories attached to those four walls, and most of them were about a part of my life I wanted to cancel out until I had recovered fully.

After some time, I found a place in a shared house in Dalston with Frank, a calm ginger Dutch guy working for a charity organisation in East London. We got along quite well, respecting each other's space as much as we could. He was not into parties, but rather Sunday roasts, vintage clothes and antiques. This helped me a lot, since that was the type of life I was going to have. I was eight months sober, and my life was in balance like never before. I kept going to my meetings and weekly appointments with my therapist, where I would discuss all aspects of my past and present life.

I felt aware of who I was, and what I wanted to be. A person that could stand on his own two feet without needing anyone to support him.

I started to have new friends, and people to spend days with at the Tate Modern, or sitting in a cafe in Stoke Newington, talking about everything without the fear of being judged. Roo, my ex-flatmate and friend, was always with me, we had bonded so well. Incredible how a friendship can build up out of nowhere and start from an unfortunate life situation.

We created a monthly calendar of things to do, searching for cultural events on the 'Time Out London' website. We kept our cinema day, and added a monthly theatre show, and Vietnamese meals in Shoreditch High Street. On Sundays, we would enjoy a roast dinner with my flatmate in Columbia Road at the Royal Oak. We would go around 1pm, because the flower market closed at this time, and you could buy Orchids for £5 instead of £12, and many other interesting things as well.

We would come back home full of food in our bellies, but also with many plants in our hands. Our house became a beautiful forest of plants and flowers, a little Eden in the middle of polluted London.

With Frank, we would talk most of the time about music: all about the new indie bands and the gigs in Rough Trade East. He was obsessed with David Bowie, and would play his songs on his guitar each Sunday evening by candlelight with a cuppa in the living room: it was our cute way to finish the week, and start the new one energised.

Then autumn arrived. Leaves were creating a magical path in Victoria Park, and the air carried the scent of hot chocolate and long afternoon teas. It was almost my birthday.

I was a new person: transformed from the messy guy I had once been. There were no major regrets about how I had lived and behaved in the past. I was aware of who I was, and what I wanted to become.

I felt my life was in balance, and everything seemed easier to deal with. In the meantime, I became manager of a tiny vintage store in East London, had many friends, and felt OK with the idea of being alone.

When I felt ready, I went to a few parties, soon realising It wasn't something I enjoyed anymore. I felt as if I was in a giant space full of lost souls trying to get attention in order to have sex, take drugs or get drunk just for the sake of saying, 'I had a wild weekend.'

There was not much judgement on my side, I had been in that state of mind not many months before, and I knew how difficult it was to get out of the vicious cycle. To those I knew, and I could see they were completely lost, as I had been, I just said, 'Mate, there is a colourful world out there waiting for you when you are ready.' Mostly they would smile at me and eventually, many months later, they would be there in that colourful world with me, confirming how right I was.

On my birthday, Frank and I decided to have a stroll in West

London, a place completely new to both of us. We took the Hammersmith line towards Kensington. The plan was to visit the Saatchi gallery and have brunch. I left the phone at home. I just wanted to enjoy that Sunday without checking my social feeds: something that was difficult to not be addicted to, but I also wanted to be free from technology.

I was 30, sober, and with a normal life. Fuck, what an achievement!

We went to the Saatchi gallery and then to a Mexican cafe where we enjoyed our brunch, watching people walking by on the street. People-watching was one of the things we loved to do. We didn't judge, but we loved to create life stories for them: who they were, their jobs, and their relationships. We laughed most of the time, as we created Hollywood-movie style stories about those people. It was a nice way to play with our imagination and be silly for a while.

Then we went back home. The day was treating me magically, and I knew nothing would destroy it, until I took my phone and saw 25 calls from my mother and sister.

I thought they were just calling to say 'Happy Birthday' to me. I knew they thought I was a mess, and I was just getting crazy with drugs and alcohol. My mother had this vision of the future with me either dead or in prison. So I decided to call her back. The phone rang for a while, and, just as I was about to hang up, my step-sister Paloma picked up the phone:

'Daniel, where are you? We called you thousands of times. Anyway, listen, we need you to come back tomorrow: dad died this morning. Cancer killed him in one week.' Everything broke down around me, and the day of clear happiness became a new nightmare to deal with.

My world went slow and messy for a couple of days until I came to terms with what was happening. No one in my family had realised that it was my birthday, which was totally understandable since my stepfather died the same day, but this made me feel uncomfortable and unloved.

I managed to find a flight the morning after the call, and arrived in the late afternoon in front of my family's door, breathing deeply, and knowing in my heart that the whole situation would be challenging. I took courage and rang the doorbell. My mother opened the door and hugged me, crying in desperation, and my sister came behind my back, cuddling my head with a cold touch.

'We went to hospital last week: your father was not feeling well. After a few tests, they found cancer throughout his body. They gave him just a few days to live. I didn't say anything to you because I didn't want to stop your life for that. These last few days were terrible. He couldn't even recognise us anymore, and now he is gone. What will I do without him?' My mother said nervously, and cried.

'We are a family; we need to stick together. Paloma and I need you here, yes, we need you here!' she added, her face changing from sad to serious.

I felt my heart falling into the ground, I couldn't believe he had passed away that fast, and with me completely unaware of everything.

We had only four days to prepare the funeral and to sort out all the bureaucracy related to the death. 'Things need to be done quickly,' my mother kept repeating.

That evening, my sister Paloma came to my room with a bottle of wine. She sat next to me, touching my shoulder, and trying to comfort me:

'I know you don't drink anymore, but you will need a glass,' she said.

Paloma filled a glass and gave it to me, and nervously I put the glass on the little desk next to the bed. She started to talk.

'You know, mum is getting crazy, but this is something we already know. I don't think that what I have to say will make you happy, but I need to tell you what happened. She didn't want me to call you last week, she felt that dad didn't want to see you after all you've done to them in the past few years. It is not fair, anyway: I am sure he wanted to see you. We had talked about coming to visit you in London later this year. He was excited to come, but mum was more concerned she might find you in a messy situation. She still goes on and on about those days you didn't call, and how they spent hundreds for the flight. But you are here now, and that is what matters.'

Yes, I was there.

Paloma is the daughter of my stepfather and my mum. 'The wanted child,' my mother would say on her drunk Sundays also pointing out that I was a terrible mistake.

Paloma and I have nine years' age difference, and this is maybe why we are totally different and not really attached to one another. She had been a good daughter, had great marks at school, and had taken part in many sports. Every Sunday, she would go to Mass, dressed as my mother instructed her to dress. We didn't get along well, mostly we argued, or had different points of view about life and how to deal with it. However, we understood each other's limits and boundaries. My mother had been a terrible influence on her, and she would always do as she was told.

'I don't understand why mum did that, leaving me in the dark, calling me just to say he died? Why does she think I am the one with a problem? What is wrong?' I said angrily.

My sister hugged me and said, 'Listen, Dan, I don't know what to say to you, but you know how mean she can be if you don't behave as she wants. I will leave you now. Tomorrow it will be a long day, prepare yourself. It won't be easy; we have to decide many things, and prepare for the funeral.

Tomorrow afternoon there will be mourning at the chapel, and all the family will be there.'

She left the room, leaving the wine there in front of me. My body wanted to drink, but my mind started to put down a list of pros and cons, and the cons were many. The pros, only one. My mind won the battle, and I took the bottle and glass, went to the kitchen, and poured the wine down the sink. The smell was divine, and the sound refreshing: that decision made me so proud that I started to smile, and after a while that smile became a laugh, and the laugh became tears of sadness.

Ghosts

Josè was my stepfather, but I was expected to consider him my dad from the moment he joined the family. My mother would tell me to call him 'dad,' and to accept it, even if I struggled with the idea for a long time. We didn't get along well: he was a conservative man born during WW2 who had lost his father in the war, and his mother was quick to lash out at all of her children.

Josè had his own ideas about living and building up a perfect life: he was a cold-hearted person, and he was emotionally absent. When he was 24 years old, he inherited the family business from his aunt. They dealt in luxury furniture in Madrid. Then, when he was 45 years old, he decided to sell everything to a large company that gave him a huge acquisition fee, after which he was able to retire.

He met my mother on one of his business trips to Brazil. My mother liked him, or at least that is what she told her family. Eventually, after 2 years of dating, he proposed, and she accepted, knowing we would have a great life ahead of us.

He was never satisfied with my school marks, He would scream to me that I would never be anyone if I could not improve my marks. Each day, my mother would come to my room and say I had to change, or she would get rid of me. She would also add that she had changed her life for me, and I had to be thankful for what I had. Everything about me was a problem for both of them.

He was a man of few words. When I came out as gay, he shook his head heavily and left the room, while my mother cried and screamed that I was the ruin of her life.

I didn't feel loved by them at all. And, to be honest with you, I didn't know the meaning of love, because I was always treated like the black sheep of the family.

When Paloma was born, my stepfather changed completely, becoming the sweetest person on earth, but only with his new daughter. Once in a while, he would hug me, but I am sure it was a gesture recommended by his therapist, whom he would visit every Monday morning. He had an obsessive relationship with his therapist, and I think it was the only place where he could take a break from all of the craziness going on in his life. By that time, my mother had started to become alcoholic, mixing alcohol with all of her prescription medicines.

When I left home at the age of 19, my relationship with Josè changed. We began to talk more, and developed more of a father-son relationship.

I would tell him about my life, and the challenges I was facing. For his part, he comforted me with sentences such as, 'I can see the world is providing you with some real meaning in your life, and I am so happy for you.'

During my darkest days in London, my family acknowledged the situation, but they kept silent. They didn't want to face up to what had happened, or help me. Because my mother was terribly ashamed, she would lie to friends every time they asked about how I was doing.

When I came home to visit them after my first suicide attempt, Josè took me to his office and said, 'Daniel, either you change and wake up, or I will disinherit you!'

I answered, 'I am not your biological son, so I don't want to be part of your shit.'

In shock, he stood up and left the office. The next day, I flew back to my drugs and alcohol.

He was not a bad stepfather, he simply had his own way of dealing with emotions, and challenging situations.

As I stood there in the kitchen, watching the wine going down the drain, my face was covered with tears. Somehow, I missed him.

In the living room, there was the chair he would sit in to listen to tales of my life in London each time I returned. Now that place was empty. His smell still lingered, even after his physical presence had gone.

The next morning, we woke up at 6 a.m. My mother was impeccable, in a black dress, and perfectly made-up.

'Daniel, I left the suit I want you to wear on your bed. I don't want you to wear that thing you have on. People talk, and I don't want them to think you are the crazy son coming from London.' She stared at me, waiting for my answer, but instead I just nodded. As much as I wanted to scream and even strike out at her, I accepted things as they were. We were all grieving, and it was better to stay calm.

We went to the bank to place all of my father's money in my mother's account, before the bank froze the account for a few weeks. We then went to the Council offices to deal with all of the paperwork. In all these offices, my mother suddenly took out a tissue from her bag and cried, saying things like, 'I don't know what I will do without him, he was the love of my life.'

The tears stopped as soon as we had left the office. Paloma and I looked at each other, puzzled by the situation, and how quickly my mother could change her emotions in front of different people.

While she went to buy a dress for the funeral, she sent me to the mortuary. She gave Paloma and I a list of things she wanted for the funeral that included white orchids, a white coffin and classical music.

The man in the mortuary said it was impossible to have a white coffin if we wanted to cremate the body. But my mother screamed down the phone that she wanted a white coffin, because it was more elegant, and in the end we had

2 coffins: one for the funeral and the other for the cremation. It was a crazy choice, but even the mortician couldn't do anything to dissuade her.

The afternoon we went to the chapel, the coffin was open with Josè's body on display. I was not ready to deal with another death in my life. Farez's death had been too traumatic for me.

My mother stopped me and said, 'Listen, Daniel, behave. All of the family will arrive soon, and I don't want either of you crying or making any sort of drama. Don't talk about your life, and comfort anyone who comes to give you a hug. This is Josè's and my moment, not yours.' In shock, I agreed. I knew my mother was mean, but not to this excess.

I went to stand by the coffin, and in front of me I saw Josè. His skin was pale, and he was terribly skinny: almost unrecognisable. In fact, for a moment I thought there had been a mix-up at the mortuary. Then I saw a particular mole on his cheek which I recognised. He wore the light blue wool suit from his wedding, a navy tie, his favourite handkerchiefs, and gold cufflinks.

A tear ran down my cheek. I looked across the room, and my mother was staring angrily at me. I took a deep breath, wiped my eyes, and went to the right side of the chapel where my sister was standing. She took my hand and said, 'you can cry tonight.'

People started to arrive. Family members and friends I haven't seen for many years were all shocked to find me there, and I didn't understand why. I just thought, 'God knows what my mother told them about me.'

Around the room, everyone was crying and embracing, saying things like, 'He was a great man. Life is not fair, but he is in a better place now.' Was he really in a better place? I asked myself, silently.

The priest came, and we started the rosary around the white coffin. I stayed in silence for the entire rosary. I had stopped believing in God many years before. Some people looked up to judge the fact I was in silence, and my mother, seeing that, took a tissue from her purse and started to cry out loud, almost screaming. Everyone went to give her comfort while she repeated, 'Why? Why? Why? How am I going to deal with life now!'

This directed everyone's attention towards her, rather than my silence during the rosary.

When the rosary was over, we said goodbye to everyone. The funeral took place two days later.

Paloma sat at the living room table and filled her glass with wine. I stood up and took a glass of water. My mother came with a glass of brandy, which had been my stepfather's favourite drink.

'I don't want to repeat myself, Daniel. I don't want people to think you are a problem child, so next time, try to scream the rosary out loud, OK? Paloma, be more comforting with people, you are better than that.'

'Tomorrow, I am going to the lawyer and notary. Your father left you $5000 each, and the rest is mine until the day I die, when what is left will become yours. We are also going to shop for a dress for you, Paloma, and a suit for you, Daniel. There will be many people at the funeral. Your father was loved, and I want people to see us at our best.'

'What about you? Will you pretend to cry, as you did today? They should give you an award for best actress.' I said.

She looked at me, and slapped my face, 'I have just lost my husband. I loved him, and I won't allow you to ruin all of this! You already ruined his life; surely the cancer came because of you!' I remained in shock for a few seconds. I wanted to slap her back, but I said:

'Mother, I will tell you one thing: I will respect you during this time of grief, but next time you try to slap me, I will ruin your life in a way no-one could imagine!'

I stood up and went to my bedroom. I was fuming, and just wanted to go back home. I called Roo and Frank, and both told me to stay calm, I would soon be back in London.

I also texted Gabriel to tell him about my father's death, and how much I missed him. He called me. He was somewhere in the US, and asked me if I wanted him to come back to support me during this grief process. I wanted him with me, but I said not to worry too much, 'Everything will be fine, but thank you for being such a great person.'

Paloma knocked on the door, opened it, then came and sat down on the bed and said how sorry she was.

'Paloma, your 'sorry' is as worthless as your mother's life. Listen, let's talk tomorrow, because I don't want to say anything I will regret.'

That night, I had nightmares about Josè sitting in a chair and saying, 'brace yourself, this is just the beginning.' I woke up confused, with my heart beating so fast I could feel it in my throat.

The next day, I called my doctor, explaining the situation I was in, and he sent me a prescription for tranquillisers by email. I went to the local pharmacy, but they couldn't accept it because it was from another country. So I cried in a dramatic way, explaining what was happening in my life, and eventually the pharmacist gave me the medicine, as he felt for me. Later that day, we went to the mortuary to discuss the final details of the funeral. My mother wanted everything to be perfect, and spared no expense.

For the entire day, I was calm and ready to deal with everything: the tranquillisers helped me a lot.

The funeral day arrived. We all dressed up. My mother inspected us from head to toe. I had a black suit with the same handkerchiefs as my father; Paloma wore a long black structured dress with a tiny white brooch that reminded me of the white orchids my father loved. My mother wore a simple black dress with a black hat and a veil, ready to cover her face and fake tears.

We took the car and went to the church. There were candles and white orchids everywhere, which to me looked more like a rock music video than a funeral.

People started to arrive, and soon the church was packed. The Mass began.

'I wrote a letter, and you will read it at the end,' my mother said, placing a piece of paper in my hand.

Confused, I said, 'yes.' I couldn't bring myself to say 'no.'

The Mass came to an end, and the priest announced, 'Now Daniel, Josè's son, will read a letter for all of us.'

I stood up with the letter in my hand, went up to the microphone, and opened it. There was an awkward silence. I was not ready to read something written by my mother. The first lines said 'Josè was a man who knew how to share love with all of us.' It wasn't true. I hesitated.

I closed the letter, seeing my mother glance at me, and began to talk:

'My mother asked me to read a letter just a few moments ago, but since it wasn't written by me, I think this will not be completely authentic.'

'Josè was a tough man, and a tough father. He grew up in an era where survival meant everything. He was a man of few words. The way he showed love and appreciation was simply by saying, 'well done.' People laughed, and I continued, 'when I was nine, he arrived in my life. I wasn't ready, I have to say, but we tried to get along as best we could. Life wasn't the best, considering the many things he had to live through when we arrived here. There were many misconceptions about him marrying a woman with a child, but in all of that, he showed great strength of character. He loved my mother and I, then Paloma came along. This changed him completely. He opened up, showed more love, and started to be less tough than before. He was a great man, and taught my family and I how to stand up tall in this world. I remember the many times he would sit down with me and say, "Life is tough, and you have to be tougher in order to survive."'

This was easy to say, but hard to do. He has left us with a huge emptiness, so suddenly, that it is difficult to come to terms with. If he were here now, I would say, 'Thank you for everything, you were the best father and husband. I know you will always be here with us, thank you for everything.'

The applause started from the back of the church. Everyone

stood up, and I went back to my bench. My mother hugged me and said in my ear, 'we will talk later.'

The funeral ended with everyone coming to embrace us. Many said, 'Daniel, you are a great son to have, Josè would be proud of you.'

We left the church and went to the crematorium for our last goodbye. I placed my hand on the coffin and said thank you. My mother and Paloma cried, and comforted one another. I just wanted to take the first flight back home.

Our house was full of people: friends and family gathered and talked slowly in hushed tones. Many people offered their condolences, and asked how I was coping with the situation. My answer was always the same, 'Thank you for being here. I am doing my best to deal with the situation,' a big smile, a hug and 'goodbye.'

I wanted to escape from that situation. There was a little buffet with finger foods and drinks. Many went to fill their plates, something I found quite sad. How in the hell can anyone eat after a funeral? Humans can be most peculiar.

My auntie started crying out loud, hugging me and screaming that the whole situation was not fair, adding that it was my turn to be the man of the house and take care of everything, and not to worry, because even if I wasn't from the same family blood, they still considered me part of the family.

I stood there speechless and just nodded, giving her a hug before I saw her go to my sister and repeat the same sentences, but adding, 'you are from my same blood, your father wanted you to be the one in charge of everything.'

Then my mother arrived in the living room, wearing a different black dress, and holding a tissue in her hand.

Some family members went to hug her, and a lady left the couch she was sitting on to make space for her. 'What am I going to do now?' she said, 'How can life be so unfair? Oh Paloma, what are we going to do?'

'Ana, you have your kids with you, they will help you with everything,' one lady said. My mother looked up at me, screaming out loud, 'Daniel has his life in London, so thank God I have Paloma with me all the time!'

At that moment, I left the room and went to the back garden. I was angry about what she had just said.

My relationship with my mother had always been tough. When I was a kid, she preferred to leave me with my nanny instead of looking after me. I think that since she lost my father during her pregnancy, she was bittersweet about having a child that looked like the man she loved. For my entire childhood, she kept saying how I look like my father, before her mood would change, and she would become sad and angry with me, slapping me without reason.

When she married Josè, she sat down with me and said that she was marrying this man in order to give me a better future, and that I should be always thankful for that.

If I happened to have bad marks at school, or if I was cheeky, she would slap me, saying, 'I already told you that I changed my life for you: be thankful, or I will ruin your life.'

When I was 19, I left home. I could no longer cope with all the emotional violence I had been living with. I kept hearing that I was not enough: my life would never amount to anything.

My mother had also started to mix antidepressants and alcohol. She was violent, and many times she would call me, saying I was a terrible mistake and that she should have had an abortion as soon as my biological father passed away.

This hurt me so much that every time heard it, I would cry for days. 'Why me?' was the question that kept coming to mind.

Every time I would visit from London, she pretended to be happy to see me, then she would leave me with my sister and stepfather, and go out for drinks with her friends.

In my darkest days, she kept saying that my life would be short if I kept doing whatever I was doing, that I was a mess, and not to come back because she didn't want people to see me skinny and disturbed.

When I came out, she stopped talking to me for three months, while my stepfather kept comforting me and saying, 'you know your mother.'

All those flashbacks kept passing through my mind while I was sitting in the back garden, trying not to cry. I was too proud to let her win her own battle against me.

'So, how are you?' my mother said, 'I asked you to do one thing, and as usual, you failed. When will you learn to respect me? People said your speech was so beautiful, and to be honest, for me, it was just a huge bag of shit.' She was angry:

'If you came here to vent your anger against me, you made a huge mistake. I will go back inside.' I said, standing up, while she took me by my arms and said, 'Sit down, I need to talk to you.'

I sat down and looked at her. She stared at me:

'I think it is time you know the truth about our past. At least you will understand what I've been through, and why I ask you to respect me.'

Mother

'I met your biological father when I was 21, while I was out with some friends having a beer at this fancy bar in Copacabana. He came to our table, asked my name, and offered us another round.

'I was quite surprised and shy. My friends pushed me to join him at his table, which I did, eventually.

'Your father was 40 years old at the time. He had the same eyes and hair you have now. A beautiful, tall man, really charming: a proper gentleman.

'We stayed there for hours sitting, talking, and drinking. He told me he had never met anyone so beautiful in his life, and that I was, for sure, the woman he was meant to be with.

'I was flattered, but I also knew that many men would say the same just to take me to their bed, so I gave him a challenge. I would only be his woman if he courted me for 4 months.

'He accepted this. He would wait for me each day after work. I used to work in the kitchen of a restaurant. I hated it, but the idea that each day he would be there waiting for me, waiting to take me to all the best restaurants and places in Rio, made me so happy. I was loved. Many times, he took me shopping. He bought me everything I wanted.

'I fell in love, and after four months he proposed, and I accepted.

'He had his own food market company that was very successful. He was a well-known socialite in the city at that moment.

'People loved him. We always had parties at our home, with many celebrities and important people, including politicians.

'Everything was perfect, I had the best life ever. Everything I wanted.

'We moved to his *fazenda*. The house was massive, with thousands of acres of land. We had dogs, cats, horses and all the fruit trees you can imagine.

'We had many people working for us, and I had someone that would prepare everything for me. Oh Clara, poor woman, she was so close to me!

'Your father had his office in the basement of the house, and he would always ask me to call him before going in there, something I didn't think about too much. I trusted him, because he was giving me the best life, and also helping my family.

'He gave jobs to my brothers, and each month I would send a large sum of money to my parents.

'Each week, he asked me to drive one of our cars full of vegetables to the other side of the town. He would say, "Ana, make sure you are always in the middle lane of the road, it is a faster lane." I didn't know much, so I respected his requests. I just drove to the place to which he sent me. Some men would take the vegetables from the back of the car, and then I would come back home, without any problems. Life was good. We travelled a lot, too. I went to many places, staying at the best hotels and restaurants.

'Then, one day during the night, the police knocked at our door. Your father said, "if they ask you anything, you don't know anything." I was extremely confused, as I really didn't know what he was talking about. When I saw the police handcuffing him, I was in shock.

'I went to the police station, and a policeman questioned me:

"Your fiancé is a drug trafficker, and you don't know anything. How is this possible?"

'I was speechless. The man I was with was trafficking cocaine all over Brazil, and I was totally unaware of everything.

'They left me after 48 hours of interrogation, mostly threatening my life and that of my family.

'One of your father's friends came and told me everything, and also asked me to help him get your father out of prison.

'I didn't know what to do. I couldn't speak with anyone. I also loved your father so much, so after a bit of hesitation, I was ready to help him escape prison.

'I didn't know the plan, but the only thing I had to do was to be in a car in front of the prison with a couple of wigs. Your father's partner gave me two fake passports, saying that my name from that moment would be Isabel, and as soon as your father jumped in the car I had to drive towards Lima, and from there, take a flight to Colombia.

'The moment arrived, and your father jumped in the car screaming, "Go now, fast!"

'"Oh baby, I am so sorry! I love you so much! I should have told you everything, but it wasn't the right time." This is what he said.

'I screamed at him. I was so angry, but so in love with him. I forgave him in seconds.

We stopped a few miles from the border in a little motel. The TV was on: on the news, they were talking about him and me, showing big pictures of us. That was scary. I called my parents saying that I was OK, and everything would be fine. I put my wig on, and glued another one onto your father's head.

'During the night, we left the motel and went to the border. They were stopping all the cars. Our names and photos were everywhere by then.

'When it was our turn, I opened my shirt buttons, showing my cleavage. The police officer took the documents, and kept looking at my breasts. I flirted with him, saying it would be great to meet after. He asked if the man behind in the car was my husband, and I nodded saying he didn't understand anything, "he is deaf" I said, "so nothing to worry about."

'The police officer was so excited by the situation that he decided to put two stamps of Ambassador's Visa on the passport, which meant we could stay or do whatever we wanted in Perù. We left the border, and the police officer left me the name of a hotel. Poor idiot, he really thought we would meet there.

'The next step was at the airport, now our names were everywhere, but at the airport, as soon as they saw the Ambassador's Visa stamps, they let us jump the queue to take our flight to Colombia.

'In Colombia, a guy in the airport gave a car to your father. We drove to Medellín and arrived at his house in Colombia.
'We were free, but all over the Brazilian news, they were talking about us. I called my sister, and she went crazy, saying the police came to her house and took her to the police station: they wanted to know where we were.

'I hung up the phone. I was terribly upset about what was happening to my family there.

Colombia became our new life. Your father told me everything about the drug trafficking, and I had to help him with it all. Eventually, Brazilian police stopped searching for us.

'Your father was a terrible drinker. When he was drunk, he would treat people badly. Sometimes he would also say things that he was not supposed to say about other drug traffickers. Unfortunately, people gossiped about it, and gave your father a bad reputation amongst the other traffickers.

'I was pregnant with you. Your father was so happy he was going to have a baby. We put a lot of effort into preparing your room: he wanted you to be a prince. Then, one morning, everything changed. A man knocked at the door and shot your father dead, then said to me, "You have 3 days to leave, or you will be next."

'I was so shocked, I could barely understand it all. Clara, our housekeeper, screamed, and my dress was covered in blood. I had just lost the love of my life.

'Over the next three days, Clara helped me to pack. I took as much money as I could, and jumped on the first flight to Lima. I was 8 months pregnant. For the entire flight, I could feel you wanting to come into this world. I prayed: Oh God, did I pray! Arriving in Perù, a doctor there said to me that if

I didn't give birth at that moment, there would be complications, but I wanted you to be Brazilian, so I took the next flight, arrived in Rio and ran to the clinic, where I gave birth to you.

'You were the most beautiful child born that day in the clinic.

'I was happy, but also deeply hurt. I had you, but I had lost the love of my life, just three days earlier.

'My sister came to the clinic after I called her. A few days later, we left the clinic and moved to her house. I contacted your father's lawyer, the only man I could trust in all of that process. He helped me to buy a house, keeping everything in secrecy for four years. In those four years, I was Isabella, Monica, Lupe, Irene. We had our house, but we had to move every three months to make sure they wouldn't find us. I was so depressed that sometimes I would look to see where you were, before realising you were right there in my arms.

'My family understood the situation, and they were always there for us. We continued to live in this way till the lawyer managed to burn and delete any documents regarding your father and I. I had my name back, and we were finally able to move to the house we had bought, but I was scared and lonely. I was fearful something would happen to you, to us. That's why I kept changing nannies and housekeepers.

'I stopped trusting everyone around me. When you were 4,

you finally had your birth certificate and all the documents I needed to go back to my life as it had been. This is the story of your father, and now you understand me: why I am always being so demanding and tough with you. The only thing that kept me going was you, even if every time I look at you, I am angered by your resemblance to your father.

'You were conceived in love, the only love I have ever experienced in my life. I did everything I could to make you happy, to make your life easier, and full of opportunities. I am the one who is always being hurt, and you don't understand that at all. I asked you to do one thing today, and you just ruined it all.'

I had tears streaming down my face. I stood up, went to my room, packed my things, and left.

*** ***

It had been 2 days since my mother told me the truth about my father, and I didn't know whether to believe her or to just accept it as another lie, and let it go.

On my way back to London, I cried. I felt as though I was always in the centre of a terrible tornado, destroying everything secure and stable in my life.

How had she been able to live with that story without saying anything to me? Why had she decided to tell me right now? Why was she trying to break me in that way? Many questions without answers passed through my mind. My phone kept vibrating. It was my mother, and then my sister. I didn't want to have anything to do with them anymore.

When I arrived back in London, Frank and Roo were waiting for me at home. They kindly prepared tons of food to eat together while watching 'Gogglebox,' the only thing that, for one hour, would let me forget what had happened only days before.

Frank and Roo both thought I was just grieving heavily, but there was more to it than that. I was incapable of saying anything to them. I was not ready to be judged or asked the many questions that even I, myself, did not know how to answer.

The days passed by slowly. At work, my mind was somewhere else. Was I really the son of a drug trafficker? Was that even true?

I just needed a break from life itself, needed to leave everything and start something new, in a new place, too.

I couldn't sleep anymore. I was living in shock, and this was the worst trauma I have ever experienced.

One morning, I called in sick at work, and stayed in bed under my duvet, staring up at the white ceiling. "What can I do now?" was the only question passing through my mind. I just felt I needed a break so badly, and I had to listen to my inner voice, now or never.

I took my laptop and searched, 'remote islands to calm your life.' There were many Caribbean and Pacific islands, all tourist destinations, and quite expensive.

Not finding what I needed, I went out to Tesco Express, grabbed milk, cereals and a bar of *marvellous creations* chocolate by Cadbury: my favourite, with all the gummy sweets in it.

I walked back home, watching people and wondering how everything around me could be running so fast, when my life was passing by so slowly.

I sat in the living room, and Frank arrived from his daily yoga classes. He hugged me, and said, 'everything will be fine.' I looked at him and said, 'Frank, I need a break from my life right now.' He looked at me in shock. 'No mate, I don't want to take my life away, I just want to go somewhere remote, where I won't have to deal with people and problems for a few months. If you are OK with it, we can sublet my room for three months or so, and in this way there will be someone helping you to pay the room and bills.' He hugged me back.

'Daniel, if that will help you, I support your idea. I will miss you for sure, you are a great friend to me, but yes, probably you need that break. No worries about the room: I will sort it all out.'

He hugged me again and left the room.

I took my laptop again and searched 'peaceful European island to live in for a few months,' and came across La Graciosa, a tiny island of 800 people in the Canary Islands, close to Lanzarote. I clicked on the Google photos and saw beautiful endless beaches, and the main and only town, Caleta del Sebo, with white houses and un-asphalted roads: one of the last remaining places in Europe without tarmac.

I looked into apartments and B&Bs: they were pricey for my budget, but still affordable. I just needed to save as much as I could. That day, I emptied my wardrobe, putting my designer clothes on eBay, and throwing the rest in a green bag to give to charity. I called work, gave my resignation, and went to sell the few gold chains I had had since I was a kid. A few weeks later, I was on a bus to Stansted with a huge backpack, ready to start the next chapter of my life. I let Frank and Roo know that I would email them from time to time. I turned off my phone because I didn't want to deal with anyone except myself.

I jumped on the plane, put my earphones on, and listened to The Wars of Drugs music to calm my mind and heart. I looked out of the window and said, 'goodbye London' for now.

Heaven is Here

'I woke up in the middle of the flight, not understanding where I was. For a moment, I thought I was on a train or something like that, and when I saw the blue sky and clouds out of the window, I had a moment of panic before coming back to real life. I was not in London anymore, but was on my way to start a new chapter in my life.

After a few hours, I could finally see a little island from the window. The weather was cloudy, but everything down there was terribly beautiful. All the houses in Lanzarote were whitewashed, part of the plan that the architect César Manrique created to make the island a special place for both people and nature.

As I was preparing the move in London, I bought a 'Lonely Planet' guide about Lanzarote and La Graciosa, and tried to learn as many things as I could. That place was about to become my new home, and I didn't want too many surprises.

I saved money for two months or so, knowing that more money would come as soon as everything I left on eBay had sold. I left Frank in charge of shipping the items.

Arriving at the airport, I took a cab to Arrecife, the main town, where I stopped to eat and buy a few things I had forgotten to get in London. In the afternoon, I took another cab to Orzola, the place where the ferry departs for La Graciosa.

The cab driver, a man in his 50s, kept advising me on places to go to eat or visit in Lanzarote, while Spanish music was playing loudly on the radio. The surroundings were just magical: white houses and endless volcanic landscapes, and the ocean, blue as ever. The sun was coming out, leaving only small wisps of cloud in the sky. He said that it was quite normal to have a cloudy early morning before the weather turned sunny. He also mentioned that there had been the *Calima* a few weeks before, an atmospheric event where the wind mixed with the sand of the Sahara turned the skies orange, covering everything with it. I looked at the Sahara Desert on my phone, being surprised that we were so close to Morocco but so far from the European continent.

The journey took around 40 minutes, through a magical landscape that kept changing, leaving me speechless for most of the time.

Orzola is a little fishing village in the remote north of Lanzarote, the only connection with La Graciosa, that was 25 minutes by ferry. A ferry passes through a strip of ocean dividing the island from Lanzarote.

The little village is very distinctive, as are all the little towns in Lanzarote, with their white stone houses and blue shutters. The wind was strong and loud that afternoon. The cab driver left me by the tiny port, wishing me a good stay. Before buying my tickets for the ferry, I sat outside a café and had a *cortado* coffee and bread and butter, something that reminded me of my childhood breakfasts.

I let myself engage with that moment, and finally scream out loud: 'I am free now!' I did not understand where I was yet. I felt like I was inside of a dream, or in a movie. Everything was so beautiful and peaceful: just what I was looking for. It crossed my mind to call my mother, but then anger and frustration touched my heart. The idea of calling became something impossible to do. I had stopped speaking to her after the funeral, and I didn't want to get trapped inside that manipulative way she had made me live for many years.

I bought the tickets and jumped onto the ferry. The ocean was slightly rough. There were many tourists wearing white linen shirts, with phones and cameras ready to take photos of the journey. I found it all quite comical: I felt as if their only focus was to take a picture and share it on their social media accounts, instead of living the experience and enjoying it.

Leaving the Orzola port and looking left, there was the most magical giant brown cliff coming up out of the ocean. It seemed painted, not even real, and there on the horizon was the little island where I would spend the next three months, with its sandy beaches and little white village on the coast.

To reach Caleta del Sebo, the ferry needs to pass through

the Rio. It seems like a river dividing both islands. On the left is Lanzarote, with Mirador del Rio on the top and the beginning of Famara beach, famous for many surfers and for its long endless white sands, and on the right, La Graciosa, with its white beach coastline and small volcanic mountains.

During the journey, I started to let all the bad thoughts leave my mind. Too much had happened in the last 5 years. I had lost people I loved, and I had had too many toxic situations to deal with. I felt this had ruined a part of me. I was so afraid of being happy, because every time I tried to enjoy the idea of happiness, something terrible would come along to destroy it.

It was not easy to deal with everything I had been through. Sometimes I thought I was crazy, until I actually put my feet down on the ground and realised I was doing great.

While my mind was running through all that, and the wind was shaking all that pain out, a tall, skinny, curly-haired man asked me if he could sit next to me. It was the only empty seat on the packed ferry. I looked at him and nodded. 'Is it your first time here?' he asked in a friendly way. 'Yes, it is. I will stay for a few months, what about you?' He smiled at me and said, 'I was born and live here.' That answer left me speechless, simply because I found it fascinating that a young guy like him was born and living in such a pleasant place. 'Oh, wow. You are such a lucky guy, I mean look at this, it is amazing!'

He kept smiling and staring at me, something that made me feel slightly uncomfortable.

'Where are you staying?' He asked. I took my journal, searching for the place where I would stay, and answered, 'Costa Sol Apartments for now, and then I will see.' He nodded and said, 'Great place, you will love it.' He stood up, smiled, and said goodbye. The ferry had just arrived at the island's tiny port. It all seemed part of another world.

There was a big square in front of the port, with a few stores selling surfer experiences and souvenirs, and a supermarket. On the right, looking towards the port, there was a little beach with crystalline waters, and the houses so close you could dive into the ocean from the window.

During the weeks before arriving, I had found a small studio in the middle of Caleta del Sebo. The owner, Antonio, promised to wait for me by the port to take me to the studio. I didn't know who he was, but I saw this tall man with a little piece of paper which said 'Daniel,' and this made me smile. For once in my life, someone was really waiting for me, and I was paying for it.

'Hey Antonio, I'm Daniel.' I said. He hugged me and said, 'Welcome to paradise, how was the journey?' while trying to take my backpack. 'No, please, I can do it.' He looked with a serious face and said, 'Daniel, you are on holiday, enjoy this, and give me that.'

I gave him my backpack, while he gave me information about everything on the island. I was barely listening because everything around me was mesmerising. I have never been to such a beautiful place in my life, and this made me terribly happy.

The entire village was unpaved, the streets were made of sand, and there were many beautiful views. We passed in front of a bike rental store where Antonio said that was the only transport on the island apart from the jeep taxis that could take me everywhere else. He showed me a little supermarket where I could buy all the basic things I needed and a bar-restaurant where I could go to eat fresh fish and drink *caña*. He was over-excited about every detail of the town, and all the excitement touched me, giving me a smile I had never before had in my life.

'Here we are, your home for the next few months,' he announced.

In front of me was a typical white building with a blue door. 'The Studio is small, but I am sure you will spend most of the time outside,' he said, while entering the studio. It contained basic wooden furniture, a bed, an old television, and a small kitchen. On the right-hand side of the room was the bathroom with a shower and a little mirror on top of a microscopic sink.

'All the house works thanks to the solar panel, so make sure you don't use things like the hairdryer because it will be too much for the panel. In the shower, the hot water has a limited time. We are trying to fix this problem, but for now it only works in this way. It is important not to throw anything in the toilet, or it will break. So Daniel, If you have any problems, you have my number, or simply knock at the door of that house there, which is where I live, and I will help you.'

I smiled, and unexpectedly gave him a hug. He laughed and said, 'Oh man, enjoy your stay!' He left the house, and I sat on the comfy bed.

I felt joyful. I was far from everyone, and this was my new world. I fell asleep and woke up around 7 pm. It was time to explore the tiny village.

It was quite warm for January. There was a gentle breeze and the sky was an intense blue. I walked through the sandy streets, finding little restaurants along the way.

There were people sitting and laughing, and I could also hear music coming from somewhere. Everything was tremendously calm and chilled. I went to the tiny supermarket, bought water, a few nibbles and a can of cola, then went to the tiny beach next to the port and sat there just enjoying the moment and place.

I still didn't understand where I was. I felt as if from one moment to the next, something would wake me up and destroy everything. I think that people who have lived through many traumatic events in the past tend to live in this way, always in fight or flight mode.

I stayed there until sunset. The sun was going down below the horizon, and all my bad thoughts with it.

I walked back home, trying to remember the streets, but they all looked the same. At first, I began to feel anxious, then I laughed and said out loud, 'Daniel, you will never have a sense of direction, so calm down.'

After 1 hour going round and round, I found the house, making sure to write the name of the street on a piece of paper for next time.

I turned on the computer, sent an email to Roo and Frank, then fell asleep.

The next day, I woke up at 6 a.m., more aware of where I was. I went out and walked toward the coastline and sat on top of a rock, dipping my feet on the cold ocean. I closed my eyes and, taking a long deep breath of joy. I was in paradise.

Slowly, the village started to wake up. I grabbed a *cortado* (which soon became my favourite morning drink) in this little café by the port. The owner talked to me, giving advice about where to visit first, and told me I should maybe take a bike, even if biking in the sandy streets was hell: it was good exercise for body and soul.

Arriving back home, I met Antonio, who gave me a bike for

my stay, saying, 'This is for you: this way you will not have to rent it and spend money for nothing.' I appreciated his gesture so much that I hugged him again, realising that I needed to stop doing that.

I took my towel, water, and nibbles, jumped on the bike, and started cycling. The bar owner was right about cycling on the sand. It was hellish, especially for someone like me who had never exercised in his life.

My first stop was Playa Francesa, the most renowned beach of the island, passing through Playa del Salado and the reefs of Las Piconas.

Playa Francesa is a white sandy beach with light blue ocean. It appeared to be somewhere in the Caribbean, also because the beach was empty, and all that space was for me. I put on my swim trunks and went into the water. The ocean was colder than ever, but I didn't hesitate much before jumping in. I felt the heaviness leave my body in one second. I smiled, and thanked Mother Nature for that.

When I was a kid, I remembered that on each New Year's Eve, my mother and I would thank the goddess of the ocean Jemanja with white lilies. As much as my family were totally Christian, we still believed in Brazilian gods and goddesses.

I was feeling so light. Everything was beautiful and perfect. I sat on the sand, letting all my senses engage with each detail of what I had around me. Then people started to arrive by the beach, and I felt it was my time to move and go somewhere else. I knew I couldn't escape from other people, but I felt I needed to stay alone as much as possible. It was my way to heal the pain I held within me.

I took the bike and went by La Montana Amarilla, a yellow volcanic mountain with Playa la Cocina next to it: another earthly paradise.

No one was there yet. I sat on my towel, took my journal, and wrote down a list of things I should do during my three months on the island. The list included snorkelling, surfing, hikes, fishing and learning about the island culture.

I looked up and saw a catamaran with many people on it. Loud music was playing, and someone with a microphone was explaining about the Montana Amarilla. I laughed, adding 'find a place that humans can't go' to my list.

The first week passed by quite quickly. I created a new routine of waking up early to have a cold swim in the ocean, having breakfast and then exploring parts of the island.

Antonio took me to Playa de las Conchas that looked out on the uninhabited island of Montana Clara: this was a place reserved for wildlife.

He also introduced me to many of his friends and family, who started to me take under their wing, inviting me to lunches and dinners. I felt lucky to experience all of that, getting to know people who had a totally different upbringing from mine. During those moments, I talked about parts of my life, explaining that I was one year or more sober and that's why they would see me drinking water or a fizzy drink.

Antonio's wife tried many times to give me a glass of their honey rum. She kept saying to me that life is one, and I should drink all the rivers of the world. I answered by reminding her I also snorted all the dust of the world. And she would burst out laughing, calling me 'Loco' (crazy).

In the meantime, I sent many emails to Frank and Roo, letting them know how it was going, and all the details of the food, beaches and anecdotes. They kept promising me that they would visit. 'It sounds like paradise!' they said.

Eventually, I began to forget everything that had happened to me in the preceding months. I thought it must have been someone else's life, and not my own. How was it possible that I was still standing after everything I had been through?

In the evenings, I would walk toward the beach with my hoodie and wind jacket. It was quite chilly, but so beautiful. I would sit, letting the sound of the waves calm my mind. It was the best way to affirm that I was alive, and what I needed was only myself and my senses in order to survive in this challenging world.

It was a true paradise, and I began to accept the fact that things in life could go extremely well if you wanted them to.

It became clear that everything that had happened to me was part of a life journey, and that these events were in the past now. I realised I should be present in the moment, and not always living the present through the lens of the past.

The sounds of the waves soothed my nights, and after a while, my dreams were about me in bright, magical places: no longer the nightmares and sleep paralysis which had plagued me in the past, making me fearful of the coming day.

I loved that place, especially the way I could find a new spot to relax and reconnect with myself each day.

One day, I decided to go to Playa Baja del Ganado, a long beach on the west coast of La Graciosa, on the other side from Caleta del Sebo. Many locals suggested going there, a place where I could relax, listening to music and writing in my journal. My journal became a place where I would fill many pages with the emotions I was experiencing. It was nice to put the way I was feeling into words.

During the journey, the tyre of my bike burst. It was 8 a.m., with no one around, and I was in the middle of nowhere. I was not lost, but I had many miles to walk.

My phone didn't work. I couldn't call Antonio or anyone to help, but I felt it was totally OK to experience being alone in the middle of the island. Many years ago, I would have freaked out, but at that moment I felt serene and happy with myself.

The sun was high in the sky that morning. It was warm. I took off my shirt and walked, carrying my bike at one side.

It was a surreal landscape, the most similar to the planet Mars that I could imagine, or at least of how the National Geographic Channel portrays it: endless fields of red sand and stones.

Music was loud in my ears: Nick Cave and Kylie Minogue were singing, 'they called me the wild rose/but my name was Elisa Day.' I closed my eyes and let the sound take control of my body and emotions, throwing the bike in the middle of the road and dancing, letting my body move through the words and the violin sound of that song.

My eyes were closed, I was dancing somewhere in the world, and that was the most beautiful time I ever had. I was in the middle of an island in the ocean letting go of everything.

My senses were all one, and I could feel tears of joy running down my face. Was this the freedom I had heard others talk about?

I opened my eyes, and on the horizon I realised there was a jeep coming towards me. I lifted up my arms, to signal it to stop.

The jeep stopped in front of me, and a guy got out, saying,

'Hey, are you all alright? Do you need any help?' I walked towards him and said, 'Hey, my bike tyre burst, I am going to Playa Baja del Ganado, any chance you can drop me closer to it?' I was sure I recognised that tall, skinny, curly-haired guy, but I was not sure from where or when.

'I am going there too, let me help you. Surely you will also need to return eventually. Let's put the bike in the Jeep.' I nodded, realising I needed his help.

'You're that guy who was on the ferry a few weeks ago, right?' he asked, smiling.

'Oh, yes, yeah. I was trying to remember where I saw you, but I was not sure. How are you? And thank you so much, I thought I would not find anyone at this time.' I shook his hand and said, 'By the way I am Daniel, nice to meet you.' He shook my hand, took my bike and said 'I am Lucas, *encantado*! C'mon' let's go!'

I jumped in the green jeep. Inside, it was messy and full of pieces of paper and pencils. There was the smell of sun cream mixed with cigarettes. He jumped in the car saying, 'sorry for the mess, just make space, nothing important is here.' I nodded, making space to sit, and moving papers and boxes on the back seat.

'Were you dancing, or was it just a vision I had?' he asked, staring at me. His eyes were a deep, pitch black colour, and he had a beautiful smile that made me feel suddenly shy.

'Oh, that,' I laughed, 'this is embarrassing, but yes, I was dancing. I was trying to let my demons leave my body.'

He nodded and smiled, 'Oh I know what you mean, what were you listening to?' he asked, while starting the engine of the jeep. 'Where the wild roses grow,' by Nick Cave and Kylie Minogue. Do you know it?' He stopped the jeep, turned his head to me and said, 'Are you serious?' he turned on the car cd player, and Nick and Kylie started to sing.

I was so surprised! How was it possible that two people were listening to the same song at the same time? 'No way! That's so weird.' he laughed, staring at me and adding, *'Hombre, que esto es destiny.'*

We both laughed in excitement. It isn't every day that you find someone listening to the same song at the same moment, not if you aren't listening to the radio. After a few minutes, a magical coastline opened up before us, and no one was there. I felt like the luckiest person on earth.

He stopped the car and asked, 'If you want, you can leave the bike in the car, and if I am not bothering you, we can stay together, and then I can take you back to town.' I was not sure I was ready to share my morning with someone else, but I felt that voice inside me saying, 'why not?'

I nodded, and he smiled back. 'I promise I won't bother you much, I love to stay in the ocean and walk, searching for treasures,' he said, winking at me.

He took his bag, and I took my rucksack and went to the beach. It was something beyond incredible. The ocean was calm, and the wind wasn't there yet to disturb us.

We placed our towels on the sand, and he took off his clothes, saying, 'I hope it doesn't bother you, but I like to stay naked.' I glanced, not sure what to answer. The last time I saw a man naked in front of me was many months before, and I was not sure how my body would react to that, but I shut out the sexual idea passing through my mind and said, 'Sure, no worries.' I was extremely uncomfortable, and his body was the best thing on earth.

'C'mon, let's swim!' He stood up. I had in front of me a tall man naked, with the smoothest body I had ever seen in my life. I tried not to think much, stood up and ran towards the water. I dived into that crystalline, salty cold water, and he followed me. I felt a strange sense of lightness passing through my veins, another great bodily sensation I promised to note in my journal later.

He dived in and screamed, *'Puta madre, que fria!* - it is cold!' I laughed out loud. He came closer to me:

'So, what are you doing all alone here?' I was mesmerised by his facial features, I couldn't focus much, everything about him was perfect. 'I am here to rediscover myself, I've had a few tough years, and needed a break from my hectic life.' He shook his head, moving his hands through his curly, black hair:

'I know what you mean, and I think you are in the right place for that. This island gives power and calm to the mind, that's why I live here. I am a painter, and this is the only place I can put down my thoughts in colour and on canvas.'

I was surprised he was an artist. I felt a sense of happiness, and smiled:

'A painter, wow! I am curious to see your work.'

He smiled and came closer to me, saying, 'Well, if you tolerate me today, I will show you my work.' I laughed, and dived into the ocean. I was happy and free.

That morning, everything was special, and different from any day I had had in many years. Lucas told me about his work, and the many galleries in Spain where I could find examples of his art. He talked about his life on the island, and how solitude had helped him to do the best painting work of his career. He was born in Lanzarote; his parents had died years before, leaving him with many properties that he rented as holiday homes. That had helped him to follow his dream and become an artist. He had never had a love relationship, he felt better alone than with someone, his mind was too artistic to engage with love.

He loved to wake up early and go to swim in the ocean, no matter the weather or the ocean temperature. That helped a lot with his mental health, he said. Even though his parents died many years ago, he was still dealing with grief and anxiety.

'It is so easy to speak with you Daniel, I normally don't share much to people, but with you it is different.' I felt happy and honoured. On my side, I felt the same, and said, 'Probably because I know what it means to be in the darkness without knowing that there is a light at the end of the tunnel. Also, that I am not judgemental and... I am a good listener.' We both laughed. I was surprised by my words and the way the situation was evolving. I liked Lucas.

'It is 12.30. What do you think? We get dressed and have a fresh lunch in town,' he asked excitedly of his own plan, and I nodded happily. I wanted to spend as much time as I could with him that day. We got dressed, jumped in the jeep, and headed towards town.

We stopped at a tiny restaurant on the other side of Caleta del Sebo. A lady, probably the owner, hugged Lucas and looked at me saying, 'Bienvenido, *encantada!*' I smiled in a shy way, introducing myself to her.

We sat at a table in front of the beach. She came with two beers, and I kindly said, 'Sorry: if you don't mind I would prefer a cola zero.' 'Please don't tell me you are not a drinker?' Lucas asked, a bit surprised. 'I am many years sober from alcohol and drugs' I said, and started to share my story.

We sat there for hours. He was mesmerised by my life story, and at some points also shocked. He kept placing his hands on my arms every time something I shared was perhaps too much. 'Daniel you are just amazing, I have never met anyone as strong as you are,' he kept repeating.

I have never felt like a strong and amazing person. I perceive myself more as someone born to suffer. Life was treating me well at that moment, but my past was a giant chaos, full of traumas and bad choices.

It was almost 5 p.m. when we stood up. He paid the bill and asked me if I wanted to see his works at his home, 'If you don't mind, I would prefer to go back home and maybe we can meet tomorrow?' I said. His facial expression changed. I could see he was surprised by my answer, and after a while he took my hand and said, 'Sure no worries, I hope I didn't say anything to hurt you.'

I hugged him, smiling. The energy between us was something magical: I could feel his heart beating. 'No, you didn't. Show me where you live, and tomorrow I will come with breakfast, what do you think?' He came closer to my ear and said, 'That's a deal.'

He showed me where he lived, which was a few streets from where I was staying. We said goodbye, and I went back to Antonio's house, hoping he could fix the tyre, something he did, while saying to me, 'I saw you with Lucas, he is a great guy, you look good together.'

Cosmic Love

I had never felt so light and calm in my entire life until that moment. I lay on my bed, understanding that I had the power to make choices in life. I should decide for myself and not for others. Everything had somehow become clear: I had a future in front of me. But first of all, I had to enjoy the present. I took my laptop and sent a long email to Frank saying I was considering staying a few months more, but it all depended on if I could find a job, since my finances were running low. I opened my journal and put down a plan for the following months that included finding a job, writing poetry, perhaps a memoir, and living each second of this life as if it was the last one I had left. This sounds intense, but it put a smile on my face. I was becoming aware of the beauty life, which was a great gift given to me by this place.

The night passed, and I woke up at 6 a.m. The sun was rising. The air outside was cold, and the wind was getting slowly stronger: something normal. As much as I didn't like the wind, I was getting used to it. Sometimes it was so strong that the sand would cover everything in its path. It was insane how the landscape could change from one day to the next. And all thanks to that strong wind that howled for the entire night.

I opened the fridge and took a few things for breakfast. I was not really sure if it was too early to knock on someone else's door, but almost before I realised, I was in front of Lucas's brown door, and I just had to knock and see.

The outside of the house was half white on the top, with grey stone tiles below. The door was strong and brown, and at the top of the door there was an old glass lamp. I knocked, and waited a few seconds. The idea that maybe it was too early crossed my mind, until he opened the door and said, 'Good morning, early man,' smiling a smile that melted my heart. 'I know, I realised it was really early just now. I am sorry if it is too early, but yesterday we didn't set a time to meet.' He hugged me and said, 'I am an early riser, come in, let's have this breakfast.'

He closed the door behind us, and I found myself on a white patio with a giant dark wood bench in front of me. To my left were many cactus plants of different colours and shapes, and on the wall, a giant abstract painting in blue colours, which reminded me of the sky of that island in the early morning. On the right was a wooden sculpture, which resembled two long hands twisted towards each other. 'Welcome to my paradise, come in and make yourself comfortable' he said, touching my shoulders.

The house was a giant loft space with an area for the living room and bed, and, in the middle, an immense area full of paintings and colours. The natural light spilled in through a long window facing the ocean. 'Lucas, wow, this house is insane. Now I understand why this space inspires you so much! Oh yes, by the way, I brought a few things for breakfast' I said, while he gave me a cup of coffee with milk. 'Yes, it is my little paradise, I built everything myself with the help of Antonio and other people from the island. You didn't have to bring anything, I already prepared. But I will put your things in the fridge for tomorrow's breakfast. Now come, let's sit here.' I laughed, saying, 'Oh, wow! 2 breakfast days in a row, are you flirting with me?' He stared at me and said, 'Who knows.'

On the table there were plates full of fruits, granola, bread, butter, and marmalade. He moved the chair and said, 'Sit here.' I smiled, saying, 'Gosh, I was not expecting this, but, well, thank you!' I felt so pleased with the whole situation. On my plate, there was a flower. 'This is for you' he said. I was speechless, no one had ever done anything like that for me. I felt lucky and important. 'OK, you are definitely flirting with me, and I am totally ok with it.'

'I might be, but serve yourself, don't be shy... Have you slept well?' he said. I took the bread and butter. The bread was warm and soft. 'Yes, I had a really good sleep. Since I moved here, I have dreamt about unicorns and many other things. And you?' I asked. He opened the marmalade and passed it to me. 'Oh yes, I always sleep well. Try this marmalade, it is from the flower of cactus, something special from Lanzarote.'

I took some and spread it on the bread. 'This is delicious, wow! I was not expecting this taste.' I said, while that sweet flavour filled the perfect moment.

'It is my favourite one. When I was a kid, I used to eat jars and jars of it. It was my guilty pleasure. Daniel, I really like you.'

I froze: I was not expecting that at all. I smiled nervously and said, 'Are you sure about it? Because I am a mess, and you said that maybe you're flirting with me.' He gently took my hand, and said, 'The best mess mother nature ever made.' I didn't know how to answer, and instead, I laughed nervously. 'Lucas, I am attracted to you for sure, but I don't want anything else, don't take that the wrong way.' He kept touching my hand, adding, 'I am a person who is honest with his own emotions, and I prefer to share, instead of suppressing everything. I know it is mad!'

I liked the way he was talking about his emotions, but I was a bit confused by my own. At that moment, they were like a rollercoaster. One part of me wanted to kiss him, and the other wanted to leave, just because I had promised myself I would no longer suffer for anyone other than myself. But at the same time, he was right. Since I didn't want much attachment, he could be the perfect way to start a new chapter, on the way I perceived love and caring.

'If I am making you uncomfortable, I didn't mean to, so instead, let me show you my work' he said. 'Wait!' I stopped him. 'I like you a lot, and I am OK with what you said. But promise me you will never fall in love with me. I know it sounds adolescent, but I want to be sure we have this deal between us.' He was silent for a minute, and then said, 'OK, deal.'

We stood up and went to the work area of his house, where he started to show me his paintings: they were powerful and astonishing, and full of colour and fantasy. Antonio was right, I loved his work.

I stopped by one with a black background, red drops of rain, and the white shape of a woman walking. 'This is a dedication to my mother. You know, my parents died in a car accident, and for a long time, I dreamt about this woman wearing white clothes, walking in the darkness while the rain was falling down…' I turned towards him and kissed his lips.

I let that moment happen, and, as much as there was part of me judging my choice, I let my heart take its own complicated journey. His lips were soft and passionate, and my hand ran through his curly hair. I felt the warmth of his body touching mine. We moved to the bed, he took off my t-shirt, and I took off his. He kissed my neck, and I let all those sensations cross my body. We got completely naked, and suddenly he said in my ear, 'I want to be in you.'

We woke up a few hours later. A sparkle of light started entering the room from the big window. We saw the ocean becoming a lighter shade of dark blue, and in the distance, the skyline of Lanzarote. He turned his face to me and started to touch my face with his fingertips, saying, '*Fue brutal*, it was amazing.' I smiled while my heartbeat grew faster. Was it love at first sight, or just the fact I had had sex for the first time in many months?

Everything about Lucas was perfect: his body, his voice, the way he talked to me. This all made me feel uncomfortable, because, as much as I had promised to not become attached to someone, I already felt as though something was happening, and I didn't want to be hurt.

'I just want to say one thing, though. I don't know how tomorrow will be between us. I am OK if we become intimate friends. I like you a lot, but at the same time, I need to learn to walk through this world on my own legs, ok?' I said, with a huge fear of being misunderstood.

He kissed me and said, 'I am OK with it, I promise you not to fall in love, and you have to promise me, too.' I felt accepted and understood: this is what I needed the most.

When I left his house that evening, I felt I was ready to deal with my loneliness. For many years, the fear of being alone made me do crazy things, and mostly hurt myself, making my mind confused, living in constant survival mode. That evening, instead, I let loneliness manifest itself, and made sure to understand where it was all coming from.

Why did I live my life in fear of being alone? Why was I so scared of loneliness? The answers came from flashbacks of my childhood. I was not listened to by my mother and other people around me. Mostly, I had to use a mask to make sure I was accepted by the world. Even if that way of living created sadness and depression, it was difficult for me to get rid of. It is incredible how childhood experience can really fuck up your adulthood. We think everything is connected to adulthood traumas, but most things can be traced back to how we spent our childhood, and the way our parents treated us. And, in my case, everything was chaos: my mother never gave me proper love, only insecurities to live with.

That night, I sat out on my doorstep to watch the stars, something I never got the chance to do in London, because of the light pollution. Here on this island in the middle of nowhere, in contrast, the sky was full of tiny little shining lights, some big, and some small. It is ridiculous how the sky is endless, and we are so tiny compared to it. I remembered when I was a kid, when my aunt came to visit us, we would go outside together to watch the stars. She used to say, 'Never point your fingers to the stars, or you will have a wart on your finger forever.' I was squeamish, and that was the best way to scare me for life. From that day forward, I stopped pointing my finger at the stars, but at that moment I opened up my hand and started pointing to the millions of stars above me. I looked at my fingers, and nothing happened. I laughed: I felt healed.

The next morning, I woke up with Lucas knocking at my door. It was 6 a.m. I opened the door, and he hugged and kissed me. 'Get dressed, we are going somewhere special,' he said.

I got prepared, and we went to the port, where he took a

little boat. We jumped in and went towards Orzola in Lanzarote.

He parked the boat in the little port, and there we took a car he rented for the day.

'I don't even know why I am trusting you in this way, are you gonna kill me?' I said, in a joking voice. He laughed loudly, which was contagious, and I laughed too. 'It is impossible to kill the most beautiful person on this earth,' he said, taking my hand. 'Man, stop being so cheesy!' I answered, while looking outside the window, to see endless landscapes of volcanic rocks.

After a while, we entered the middle of the island, and I read 'Haria' on a road sign. Palm trees and colourful plants were all around this tiny whitewashed village. It seemed an oasis. Haria is a microclimate area of Lanzarote, and this made it quite easy for Manrique, the architect who created the urbanisation of Lanzarote, to plant many palm trees, making this place a special part of the island.

We stopped and parked the car. We went to the centre of town, where we sat and took a *cortado* in the only open bar at that time. On the main road, people were erecting market stalls. It was Saturday, their market day. Above us, birds and parakeets were singing out loud. I closed my eyes, and let the sound fill my soul.

'The plan is, we wait for the market to open, and in this way, you can see what the artisans do here on my island. Then we will grab some food and go to the Mirador Rincon, and later to Famara, where we can surf if you want, or simply stay there by the beach. Afterwards, we will have sex in the great outdoors.' I looked in shock, and started to laugh, 'Oh wow! The last bit of the plan, what can I say. It is perfect for me.' I said.

As soon as the market opened, we walked through it. He held my hand, and stopped at each stall to say hi to the owner, and to introduce me. He bought me an ethnic necklace made of black volcanic stone with a round silver plate in the middle: something I wore for the entire day.

We grabbed some fresh bread, *jamon* and *tortilla*, then we jumped in the car and went to the Mirador. There, we found the most magical landscape: it seemed painted, with its high mountains, cliffs and Famara beach, and the ocean a light blue mark in the midst of this perfect scenery. It is difficult to describe the beauty of the place. It was like a scene from a movie, with all those rocks, and the endless landscape spread before us.

While I was watching the view, mesmerised by it, he came and hugged me. He kissed my neck, and after a while we had sex there, still watching that enchanted view.

We took the car and went towards Famara beach, where we rented a surfboard, and he tried to teach me how to surf. It took me a while to learn, but eventually I managed to ride some waves. He cheered every time I held my body above the surf, screaming, *'Qué orgullo* — I am proud of you.' I felt powerful, and happy to be trying something new.

Exhausted, we sat on the beach, letting the sun tan our skin, while I questioned him about all the technical aspects of surfing. I was terribly excited about it. He kissed me each minute, saying, 'You are so damn beautiful!' I laughed shyly, saying, 'Stop, or I will believe you!'

We then went to La Santa, a local fishing village, to have something to drink. During the journey, we stopped in the middle of nowhere and had sex again. We were so passionate, I liked him terribly! But I kept promising myself not to let my emotions intrude into this relationship.

In La Santa, we sat in a bar, where I took a sparkling water, and he, a beer.

'I am still shocked that you don't drink anything more than water, juice and cola,' he said, 'are you never tempted?' I was tempted, but I knew that it would only ruin my life. I smiled, 'I won't lie to you, sometimes I want to have a big glass of white wine, but then, every time, I remember how messy my life was with alcohol and drugs, and I say no. Addiction was a big problem for most of my adult life, probably the worst part of it, and I don't want to go back and make the same mistakes all over again. It took me a long time to get sober, and to respect myself, and I don't want to ruin all of that just because of stupid temptation. Saying that, I don't judge anyone else who drinks, I just don't allow myself to go back there.'

He stared at me with his deep black eyes, and smirked, 'OK, so let's do this. After this beer, I promise I won't drink any alcohol in front of you. I think it is not fair to tempt you in this way, but in return for this favour, we will have to have sex many times a day.' I chuckled into my water and laughed loudly. 'That's totally fair: pinky promise, then'. He crossed his pinky finger with mine and said, 'OK, let's go: I am horny, and I want to have sex right now.'

I don't know how many times we stopped during that day to do something sexual. I was shocked at the way my body was constantly asking for him. It had never happened before. It was a powerful energy we were creating, and I was extremely excited to share that with him.

Before sunset, we took the boat back to La Graciosa and went to have our mocktails in a little bar where a man was playing music with his Spanish guitar. There were a couple of people dancing too. Lucas stood up, took my hands, and said, 'show me your Brazilian moves.' I hesitated for a moment, then overcame my fears, and got up there in the middle of the crowd to dance with him, and suddenly everyone was up, dancing and singing.

We danced till late: we laughed and enjoyed the moment. I felt like part of life, that I belonged to a world that I had never been in. Everything was calm and clear in my mind, and I could feel I was powerful enough to choose my own path in life, and to completely close the door of my past, and open up the gates of my future.

That night, we slept together, waking up and having sex in the middle of the night. Oh yes, we smelled of passion and love!

It was my second month, and I had one more to go. I started to work in a little bar for a few euros: it was not enough to survive for a few months, as I thought I could. I met with Lucas every day, having sex as often as possible. Many times, he took me around La Graciosa and Lanzarote to explore both islands. In the evenings, we would go to his place, where he would paint, and I would write articles that I sent to different blogs and newspapers, hoping to find a remote job that would give me the opportunity to stay there.

He would put music on loud, Lianne la Havas, Janis Joplin, Monica Naranjo, Juanes and Solange, and in the meantime, we would dance naked, letting our bodies eventually become one.

I couldn't control my emotions anymore: I felt like more than simply a friend with benefits.

Every time we were together, my heart would beat so fast: was this love? Yes, it was.

Each day, Lucas would prepare a surprise for us, that made

me even more confused about my feelings. I let him do it. I loved his way of living life, and love.

Each morning after sex, he would prepare breakfast, dancing, pretending to be a sexy dancer (which he wasn't) I laughed so much. I was in love with him.

With only three weeks left of my stay, anxiety started to kick in. I began to have sleepless nights, and moments of deep sadness.

One early morning, I woke up and sat on the outside patio, starting to cry. Flashbacks of my past life and my mother's situation started to crowd my mind. I was not ready to go back to that insane place again. I was terrified to lose what I had created here, including the relationship with Lucas, which was developing well.

I didn't want to go back to London and live that same life pattern that had broken me for many years. But I had no choice.

Lucas opened the door and came close to me, '*Amor, qué haces?* — Why are you crying?' he hugged me tightly. I cried more, 'Lucas, I need to say something to you. I said I would stay for a few more months, but my finances are running low, and the job at the cafe is not providing enough for me to stay and live here. I have to return to London, and I have just three weeks left here with you. I am sorry I didn't say anything to you, but I thought I would somehow manage to stay here for longer.'

He stood up and went back home. I was speechless, thinking he was mad at me, but he came back, opened my hand, and put a pair of keys into it, saying, 'Daniel, this is our house now, you don't need to leave. I will take care of you if you want.' I instinctively hugged him saying, 'I love you,' and he kissed me, repeating, 'I love you too.'

That morning, I made a Skype call to Roo and Frank. I had to share the news with them.

'I will stay here. Lucas is an amazing man, and he promised I can stay here without any problems. I will still work for a few euros at the café, but I won't have to deal with rent or anything like that. I feel so happy here, and he is an amazing guy to be with. He says he loves me, and I love him, too'.

On the other side of the camera, Roo shook his head, and said, 'Dan, you know how much we care about you, and we are happy if you are happy. But I want to remind you what you told us to tell you next time you fell in love with someone. Don't go there, or you will get hurt. We don't want you to suffer the way you did in the past. We know love is a big thing for you, but you can love yourself without waiting for someone else to love you.'

I was so disappointed, I thought both of them would be happy for me, but they were worried, and in my mind, I felt they were more jealous than really understanding the situation. 'After everything that has happened to me, I thought you would both understand, instead of looking at me and judging the situation. Guys, why are you not happy for me?'

Frank looked at me and said, 'Look, Daniel, do what you want. We said we are happy for you if you are happy. We just told you what you told us to tell you in case you fell in love with someone. You're adult enough to deal with whatever you want to deal with. If you are happy, we are happy, but if it doesn't work out, we are here. I need to return to work: talk to both of you later. Bye.' Roo said 'bye' too, and I left the call feeling heartbroken.

I felt betrayed and misjudged by my two best friends. I couldn't understand why they weren't happy for me and my decision to stay on that island with Lucas.

I knew in my heart that it was their way to take care of and protect me, but I also wanted their support in this step I was taking. I felt changed and ready to follow this new life chapter with all the pros and cons it presented. But I also needed confirmation that I was doing the right thing, and I couldn't have it by myself.

I was in love, but I also felt loved and important as never before.

In that same week, I packed my things, cleaned the house, and gave the keys back to Antonio, to whom I gave the news about me and Lucas. He was beyond excited, I was like a

brother to him, and he just wanted my happiness:
'Daniel, Lucas is an amazing person, and you deserve all his love' he said. I hugged him and started to cry, tears of happiness.

Lucas started to empty a few spaces in the house that would be just mine, and we promised we would respect one another's space, and the moments we wanted to be alone creating art, reading, writing, or simply being one with our emotions.

Each morning, we went to have a swim in the cold ocean. It was our special healing moment to start the day in a powerful way. This was a new routine that helped me to feel more grounded and conscious of what I wanted.

Lucas and I spent most of our time talking, sharing life experiences, having sex and creating art. I eventually managed to find a remote job for an online tourist magazine, writing articles about the best places to visit and eat in Lanzarote and La Graciosa, the best tours, and many other things.

Life was treating me well, and this helped me to forget all the issues I had been through, including the situation with my mother and her story about my biological father.

I also changed my phone number, which stopped me receiving any calls from my mother and sister. I would never answer those calls anyway.

A few weeks later, I received a card from Roo in the post, wishing me the best in this new journey. 'I am always here for you' he wrote. That awareness that he was always there for me made me happy. It was what I wanted to hear in the first place, but apparently, he had needed to collect his thoughts first. That same day, I sent a long email to him. I was thankful for that gesture, and I invited him and Frank to visit me as soon as they could. I just wanted them to see where I was and how I was different from the addicted, crazy guy they had dealt with in the past.

One day, Lucas woke up and blindfolded me, saying there was a surprise for me. 'So, the journey will be long, but promise me to never take your blindfold off?' he asked, and I nodded. I was extremely excited and curious about this surprise.

We walked for 10 minutes, with me asking questions about the surprise, then we jumped on a boat where he played classical music from his phone, saying, 'trust me, and don't take the blindfold off.' I smiled, knowing in my heart that I didn't have much choice but to trust him. Yes, I loved him, and the relationship was all about support and trust. I started to laugh nervously. I just wanted to understand what the surprise was for.

We stopped, he took my blindfold off, and in front of us there was a little dock full of flowers, and a table in the most amazing landscape you could ever imagine.

We jumped off the boat, and Lucas took my hand, saying, 'I have something to tell you. I have never been this happy in my entire life. For a long time, I thought I would never find anyone to share my life with, and now I've found you, and I know I will never be alone. Now let me tell you that you don't have any choice, since I've already prepared everything,' he laughed.

I felt my heart racing, I wasn't prepared for that experience, because no one had ever been romantic to me in that way. 'So here we have a table, two rings and the ocean in front of us. I want this moment to be ours, and I want this nature to marry us right now.' His voice was soothing and full of passion. 'So, you are asking me to marry you, and nature will be our priest?' I asked. 'Yes, I want this moment and this exchange to be our symbolic way to say to each other that we belong together no matter what, and we will always be together.'

I cried, and kissed him. He took the ring and placed it on my ring finger saying, 'I promise I will always be here for you, to love you for my entire life, and to support and give you the happiness you deserve. The ocean is here to testify to this moment that will be always part of us.' I took the ring, placed it on his finger, and said, 'Wow! I was not expecting all that. I promise I will always be next to you, and I will always support our relationship and our love, and ocean you are here testifying this moment and if you fuck up, I will throw you in the ocean!' We laughed, kissed and hugged. That was really a moment that will always stay in our hearts, minds and lives.

After that moment, he went over to the catamaran his friend had lent him and took some food, then we had breakfast at the table overlooking the ocean. 'I used to come here every time I felt alone. Yesterday, I came and prepared everything, hoping the weather wouldn't ruin it all. Now this place no longer represents loneliness, but rather, love' he said. 'So, you're telling me that yesterday while I was working, you came here to prepare everything?' He smiled and nodded. 'And at home, I have another surprise for us.' 'Another surprise? You're trying to make me cry on purpose, aren't you?' I said. His eyes were giving me all the love I needed. I felt I was part of a movie; my past life was made of suffering, and now it was all about joy. How was this possible?

When we arrived home, on the patio there was a Labrador puppy with a red bow around its neck, which was Antonio's gift for us. He had helped Lucas to prepare everything the day before, and the puppy was his gift for this new chapter in our life.

After a long discussion about the name of the puppy, we decided we would call it Hector. Hector the brown Labrador.

I had a family at that moment, a family made of love and support, something I had never had before.

Ship to Wreck

Lucas's paintings were exhibited in many galleries throughout the Canary Islands, and also in Spain. People loved his paintings, and many were sold to wealthy people all over the world. It was so powerful to see him painting: he would sit down on the floor, closing his eyes and breathing deeply before opening his eyes, and starting to throw colours with brushes, his fingers, and many other tools. Music helped him a lot during this process. A process during which no one was allowed to talk to him.

One day, he received a call from a gallery owner in Madrid. They were creating an exhibition about the greatest new Spanish artists, and they wanted him to be part of it. That evening, we celebrated with all his friends and local people from the island. Lucas and I broke our promise, and we both drank a little glass of prosecco. I broke my sobriety, but I also knew it was something of that moment, and that I would never drink anything again. As much as I wanted to drink more after the first glass, I just reminded myself I didn't need it.

Drinking that little sip made me remember the past, and I had to take a moment far from the party celebration to let all those thoughts leave my mind and body.

Lucas came to find me '*Amor, non te preocupe*: Don't you

worry, that glass means nothing, and you are stronger than that. I am here with you, and you are not what you used to be. Let it go.' I sweetly smiled at him; he was right. I was a new person now, and I would never go back to who I had been.

The next day, Lucas received his invitation, and flight tickets to the exhibition. He would pay for the whole trip for me, but I felt guilty about him doing that. 'I know you want me there with you, but I don't want you to spend that money for me. This is your moment, and I want the lights to be on you alone. Plus, I have Hector here with me, so nothing to be worried about. I will miss you a lot, but at the same time it will only be five days, and it will pass quickly.'

At first, he was disappointed, but he also understood my point. At the end of the day, during the three events they were doing there, I would be mostly by myself since he would be extremely busy with all the networking activities.

One week later, I took him to the airport to catch his flight to Madrid. We hugged for a few minutes. I wanted to cry, but I didn't want him to feel regretful of his decision. After he left for the security check, Hector and I headed to Tinajo market. I wanted to keep as busy as possible, so I wouldn't think about it.

I tried as hard as I could not to let the feeling of being alone and missing the one I loved take over, but it was difficult. When I came back home, I threw myself upon the bed, hugging the pillow that smelled of Lucas.

The first night, I felt lonely as hell. I cried during the night. I felt confused by the idea of not having him around.

I was reacting to the situation very badly, and I didn't know how to deal with it in a positive way. I knew I was sinking into a deep depression, but it was the only mechanism I had to deal with something being completely out of my control. For all those months, I had had Lucas there, and now being there by myself made me feel I was not strong enough.

Lucas arrived safely in Madrid. He called me many times that morning, just to make sure I was OK. I wasn't, but over the phone, I assured him everything was fine. Our calls were quick because he was busy from the moment he arrived.

I took the jeep and went to the beach with Hector, who was strangely attached to me. He could feel something was off, and wanted me to be calm and happy as I was when Lucas was there with us.

That afternoon, I tried to call Lucas many times, but mostly he answered with, '*Amor, qué te llamo más tarde*, I will call you later. I am busy,' and that broke me terribly.

I was not ready to understand the fact that someone was busy, and not 100% of the time with me. I started to remember all the past relationships, and how some of them ended with less phone calls and texts, to completely ghosting each other.

That idea created anxiety in me. And I began to be nervous, biting my nails until they bled. I went to work in the bar, and had a breakdown in the toilet. I didn't know what was going on, but I was reminded of Farez's death, and I felt terribly alone. With hindsight, I was definitely overreacting, but at that moment it was the only way I could live. As soon as I finished my shift, something changed in me. The old demons took over my mind, and there was nothing I could do to get rid of them.

I left work and went to the supermarket, bought a bottle of rioja, and went back home. I played Florence and the Machine's 'Ship to wreck,' and opened the bottle. I knew deep in my heart that what I was doing was wrong, but I also felt it was my only way to escape from that suffering. Hector was staring at me and I said, 'don't judge me, I promise it will be just one bottle.'

I started to drink, feeling light, but at the same time, terribly sad. By the second glass, I was already drunk. The phone rang. It was Lucas. 'Hey, sorry for today, but I had many interviews and other things. I really miss you. How was your day?' he asked. I drunkenly answered, 'Well, I had a terrible day, I feel you don't love me anymore, and this is a problem.' There was a strange silence, and after one minute he asked, 'What are you talking about? I love you, and you know that.' I no longer had proper control of my behaviour, and I said, 'Do I really know it?' I drank another sip, burped down the mic, and finished the call.

The phone kept ringing, and I passed out, waking up the next day with the worst hangover I have ever had, and with 50 missed calls and many messages on my phone.

I called Lucas back, almost unable to remember anything I had done or said. 'Why are you doing this to me? I spent the night awake and afraid for you. Fuck, Daniel, I love you, and you can't play in this way with me!' he said with an angry voice. I was in shock, looking at the empty bottle of wine on the floor. I felt so ashamed. 'Babe, I am sorry, I don't know what to say, other than "sorry." I felt so alone, and I stupidly drank. I promise it will never happen again, I am such a terrible kid. Sorry.' I was heartbroken, why was I behaving in this way?

'Listen, I need to go now, in two days I will be there, and we will talk about it. Please don't do anything stupid, I really care about you, and I don't want anything to happen to you and to us.'

We put the phone down, and I felt horrible and heartbroken. In my NA meetings, many years before, there was this man that had been sober for many years, and one day out of nowhere started to go back to drugs and alcohol. Was that happening to me, too?

I called my therapist, who was surprised by the call, since I'd been out of therapy a long time. We arranged a video call in which I talked about what had happened, and the only thing she said was, 'Trauma can be a gun if you don't pay attention and heal it.'

I thought I was through with my traumas, but apparently I had drunk again just to forget.

Those two days before Lucas's return were the worst I had ever experienced. I started questioning all my choices, and my relationship with Lucas. Was I using him as an anchor, in order to be saved? Was I covering my pain with his love? Was I truly happy? All those questions kept popping into my mind, as well as many flashbacks to my childhood: my mother's behaviour and attitude; my stepfather's death; Javier, Jacob and all those people that unconsciously hurt me, and took advantage of my weak mind and life.

From one moment to the next, my life went back to the chaos of the past. I needed to find the right solution, knowing that maybe the choice would ruin what I had created up to now.

After those two days, I picked Lucas up. We hugged for many minutes, with him placing my hands on his heart and saying, 'can you feel this? I can't live without you. You are the person I want to spend my entire life with, and I am here to support you.' I felt horrible, and went in a terribly silent mood.

During the journey back, he talked about the exhibition,

and all the connections he had made in Madrid. He told me that business would grow: they had promised him different exhibitions at various galleries in Spain and the UK. I was happy for him, and afraid of myself.

That night, I woke up, left the house, and walked to the tiny beach we had in front of it. I sat on the sand and looked to the sky. The moon was high, and all the stars were brightening.

I felt my heart tighten, unsure of what I should do, and how I could stop being that way.

After a while, Lucas sat next to me, taking my hand and saying, 'everything will be fine, don't let yourself overthink. You haven't done anything bad, and I am always here for you. A bottle of wine does not define the person you are. You know and I know that is not you.'

I looked at him and said, 'I love you more than anything in this world, but I am afraid of me. When I came here, it was because I wanted a break from my hectic life, and I wanted to reconnect with myself, firstly. Since I met you, my life has changed for the better, but I think that what I've done is cover all my insecurities and fears without even going there and touching them. I don't want to ruin us, and you. These last few days, I really thought about my future, and our future, and I want to start all of that in the right way.' I took a deep breath, 'I need a break from you, to understand what I really want. I can see my future with you, but at this present moment, I need to see me first.'

In shock, he stood up and said, 'What are you talking about? Do you want to break up over a bottle of wine? *Amor, por favor!* baby — don't. I can't be without you. I will give you everything you need, but please don't leave me.'

'And that is the problem I am talking about. We have to learn to be apart before being together. I will collect all my things, and I will leave tomorrow. I love you, and I am sorry.' He turned and left. He didn't come back home that day, and the day after I took a few of my possessions, and left a letter:

Lucas,

I am destroyed by my choice. I really don't want to hurt you, as I am probably doing now.

During these last few days, I really thought about us, my choices, and where I am right now in my life, and I realised that I spent most of my time concealing my problems so I wouldn't have to deal with them. But the more we uncover, the more that comes to the surface, and during these days alone, I felt that something was off, and life crashed in front of me. I have never been so happy in my life as I have been with you, but you deserve someone balanced and self-assured that will never hurt you as I can do right now.

I love you, God, I do, and all this hurts me badly, but I need to take a moment for me. You see it as an end, but this is not our end. I am going to Lanzarote to stay in a B&B. Give me a few days: promise me to respect my choice right now.

On the ferry to Lanzarote, he tried to call me several times, but I didn't answer. I didn't know what to say, and freaked out. When I arrived at my B&B, he was there. He had managed to find out where I was through Antonio, with whom I had talked that same morning.

He was visibly destroyed: his eyes were swollen. He had probably cried all day, and that broke my heart still further.

'Daniel, don't leave me. I understand what you are going through, but you can't leave me this way. I can't be without you. I am lost, I can't breathe. I am here to support you!' he said crying, touching the ring we had exchanged, 'I will do everything you want me to do. Do you want time, OK? I will give you time, but don't destroy us.' He said.

'Lucas, I just need this time for me, please,' I said, asking him to go.

Why was I like that? Why was I always ready to ruin the best things I had in life?

I was so confused, and not sure of what I really needed at that moment. That evening, I went by the cliffs of Arietta. I went through all the moments I had almost ruined mine and other people's lives. I ruined every relationship I had ever had.

I was never happy, and unconsciously I would end up being obsessive, and they would leave me in desperation. My friend Farez died because I didn't stop him taking drugs, my stepfather died because he was ashamed of me. My Mother was horrible to me because I reminded her of the man she used to love.

I felt as though I was a huge failure, I didn't deserve to have a life.

I walked by the edge of the cliff, feeling the breeze of the ocean caressing my body. I felt heaviness in my shoulders, while the moon illuminated what was going through my mind. I had only one thought: 'Jump, that will save you from suffering.'

I closed my eyes, breathed, and the phone started ringing persistently. I didn't want to answer. I wanted to jump and finish everything.

But the phone kept ringing persistently: an unknown number. The first thing that passed through my mind was that maybe Lucas had harmed himself, so I picked it up. 'Daniel, it is me, Paloma. You have to come back: mom is dying.'

I was silent for a moment before answering, 'OK.'

That evening, I called Antonio and explained the situation. He lent me the money for the flight. 'Antonio, please take care of Lucas and Hector for me.' I said.

Kiss with a Fist

On the flight back to my mother's house, I felt as if my heart was stopping each second. As much as I was resentful of my mother, I still had feelings. At the end of the day, she was my mother. I couldn't face the fact that everything was so confused in my life, and how in one week, everything I had created had crumbled in such a terrible way. Now, my mother was dying. How could I face any further grief, when I felt I had no strength left in me?

During that flight, I kept my sunglasses on. Tears were running down my face, my emotions were overflowing, and I felt as though I was exploding.

In my mind, there was chaos: Lucas, Farez, my father, and now my mother.

As much as I hated my mother for what she had done during my stepfather's funeral, I felt my heart contracting, knowing that my last words to her had been in anger, as the result of an argument. I had walked away, and ended our mother and son relationship.

Throughout my childhood, as much as she was restricted and without much love to share, she had been my mother. Growing up in a Catholic environment, you are supposed to love your mother, no matter what.

It is strange to hear a son or daughter saying they do not love their mother, isn't it? It sounds like a terrible sin. 'How can you not love your mother? Are you crazy?'

Did I love her? No, I didn't, but I cared about her. When I moved to La Graciosa, my intention had been not to talk to my family for a long time. I needed to recover before facing any further family drama. They made me feel sick, and I couldn't cope with all the lies I had lived with for so many years.

For many of the important moments in my childhood, my mother wasn't there. My first day at school, my aunt came to pick me up because my mother was busy at the hairdresser. At my first school recital, no one was there: she forgot about it.

But at the same time, that was the only love I knew existed. She was the one I had copied in order to survive in this world. She was the only one I could rely on throughout my lonely childhood.

At the realisation she was now dying, I sensed a huge emptiness touching my world.

I felt alone again.

At the airport, I received a message from Paloma saying she couldn't pick me up, and because of that, I had to take the bus home.

I was drained by everything. I tried to call Lucas, but it seemed he had blocked my phone number. Then I sent a message to Antonio to let him know I had arrived safely.

I jumped on the bus. The journey was long: it was two hours from Valencia airport. I fell asleep and dreamed about living another life where there weren't any problems and difficult challenges to face. I was smiling and calm, and had Lucas next to me, even though I couldn't see his face. There was a river separating us, and in the sky, the figure of my mother throwing stones at me: she wanted me dead. I woke up suddenly, not understanding where I was. It took me a few moments to realise why I was there, sitting on that bus. A few stops later, I was at my mother's home.

I wasn't at all ready to deal with death once again, so I prepared a plan in my mind, in which I would say sorry to my mother, and stay with her till her last breath. She had done so much for me, and that was the only way I could say thank you without hurting the both of us. I also promised myself that I would take many breaks during those future moments, so as not to not break my already broken self still further.

My stop arrived. I prepared my rucksack, and looked at my face reflected in my mobile phone screen. I was tired. Oh yes, I was tired.

Walking toward my mother's house, my heart started to contract. How could I cope with all this grief alone, again?

I know that Paloma and I were supposed to support each other, but at the same time, I didn't want her support at all.

I cried, drying my tears with the sleeve of my shirt. I arrived in front of the door and rang the bell. Paloma opened the door, and this left me shocked, 'I thought you said you were not at home.' She hugged me, 'Mum is coming, she will arrive soon.' I looked at her, confused, 'from where? Is she OK? Why is she not here?' I asked. Paloma couldn't look me in the eye, and that rang alarm bells for me. I felt something was off.

'I've put some towels in your room, go and have a shower' she said, leaving the room.

I went upstairs and had a shower, crying. I felt dead inside. I knew there was something abnormal about Paloma's behaviour.

I ran to the toilet and puked. Panic had taken hold.

I heard the house door opening, put on some clothes, and went downstairs.

My mother was sitting in the living room. She looked perfectly well to me, and that left me speechless. 'Daniel, my son. You are here.' She stood up and gave me the biggest loving hug I had ever received from her.

'Mum, are you OK? What is going on?' I asked. I had a cold

sensation running through my body: she didn't look sick at all, but at the same time I didn't know what was wrong with her, that would cause her to die soon.

She kissed me, 'Daniel, I am OK. I just wanted to talk to you, since you stopped answering my calls, and changed your phone number.'

I had never felt so confused in my life, and clearly my face was showing all that. She continued:

'I know you are in shock. The only way I could talk to you was to tell you I was sick and dying. Paloma helped me with the rest. You look so tired, why don't you go to have a nap, and we will talk later?' She left the room quietly.

I walked towards her, stopping her from leaving:

'So, you're saying you are not sick at all, and you lied just to get me here, so you could talk to me? Are you out of your mind? I spent the journey trying to deal with your imminent death, and you are telling me all of that was fake?'

She looked at me. I could see no shame or remorse in her eyes in spite of all my questions. 'Yes, I needed to speak to you after what happened at Josè's funeral. I am heartbroken to know I hurt you, and I want to fix everything before it is too late.'

I felt so angry. The only thing I wanted to do was punch her in the face.

'You are a selfish bitch, what do you want to fix? The fact you lied to me, and you are still lying? Don't you think it is too late to repair all of the damage you've done?' I said, angrily.

She came closer and slapped me in the face, 'I am your mother, and you should show respect, you are better than that.' I instinctively slapped her back. My anger at that moment was out of my control. I felt sick, 'I said to you already once, never touch me again, or I will kill you.' My voice was trembling, and I felt it was my moment to open up and say everything I had been through because of her.

'You are a worthless mother. I spent my whole life trying to understand why I was always a failure in your eyes, but now I can see that you are the failure. You are a liar, and you keep lying to those that love you. Don't you see that? Oh, you can't, because you are a selfish bitch!'

She was in shock, touching her cheek with a trembling hand. She probably hadn't expected such a reaction from me. She tried to open her mouth and say something, but I stopped her:

'No! Shut up! It is my time now: you have already talked too much in this life. You have ruined my life ever since I was a child. You were never there for me, and you never accepted me. You told me how proud you were, and instead you preferred to hide the gay son with problems from everyone around you, when in fact, you are the problem. You are a terrible mother. You are manipulative, and you think you can get everything you need with your martyrdom and Bambi eyes. But I don't care anymore how you feel, because I hate you. I tried to love you, but you failed big time as a mother, and as much as you think Paloma loves you, she hates you more than I do. You ruined all my choices and everything I created because I spent my whole life trying to be something for you and now,' I sneered, my hands were shaking and tears were falling down my face, 'you are the one no one will ever care about. I really wish you were dead right now. Instead, you are here in front of me: you are cancer, but I will make sure I kill this cancer. The fact is, you are a horrible mother, and a terrible liar. This is the last time I will allow you to do this to me, and now you can go fuck yourself.'

She was in tears, and speechless. I left the room. Paloma was there behind me, 'I am sorry Daniel, she threatened me, and I didn't know what to do.'

'Don't come here and play the victim card with me, Paloma. You had a choice, and you chose to behave as her. A family of selfish cunts,' I screamed out loud as I left the house.

I just wanted to disappear. I didn't want a family such as this one. I took my phone and called Frank and Roo, but they were both busy, and promised to call me later.

Then I texted Lucas, 'I really need you now.' I waited a moment before realising he really had blocked me.

I was there in the middle of the road, so I closed my eyes, and a few moments later I opened them to the sound of a car horn, and a man screaming, 'Do you want to die, dickhead?'

I lifted my left arm in a gesture of apology, and went to the pavement. Yes, I wanted to die, but at the end of the day, that wouldn't change the situation I was living through.

I walked for miles, trying to collect myself in the midst of that confusion. I needed clarity, and everything was too foggy in my head. The only option I had was to go back and talk to my mother. I couldn't allow her to ruin the rest of my life. My whole life was a lie. I knew it, but I couldn't allow myself to be ruined by the pain.

So I went back, and there in the kitchen was my mother with a glass of wine, and another empty glass waiting for me.

'I am sorry! I am sorry if I slapped you! I did not mean to harm you, but it was my impulsive reaction' I said, filling the wine glass with water. I promised myself that from that moment, I would never fall into the same old habits.

'I know and understand. That's OK, I didn't mean it either. But we have to speak,' she said, with a sad look on her face. I nodded, and she started to speak:

'Daniel, I know how much I hurt you when I told our real story. I should have told you many years ago, but I was living with terrible shame and fear. There is also the fact that our past wasn't the easiest to talk about. It was difficult for me to live through it, and most of the time I just wanted to delete it. How could I say to you in your teenage years, 'Hey, you are the son of a drug trafficker.' I laughed nervously. I felt that was just insane. She continued, 'I tried my best to not come out with something that would hurt your feelings, but I failed. And I am aware I failed as a mother, too, but tell me which mother doesn't fail? We raise a family, trying not to repeat our parents' mistakes, and in the end, we do even worse than they did.

'I am sorry if you feel I was never there for you. You know I was there, but in my own way. And my harsh attitude was just my way to push you to keep going. I think now is the time I tell you everything, without hiding anything. You deserve to know the truth.'

I felt another explosion within my body. My shoulders were stiff, and my heart was in my stomach. 'The truth about what?' I asked, my hands shaking.

'Everything I've done for your entire life was to protect me and you. You don't remember, but in your childhood, we changed homes and names for many years, and that was because I didn't want all those bad people to find us. I was the mistress of your biological father and not his wife, as I said to you. I spent the entire relationship hiding, even if his wife knew everything. As soon as your father proposed to me, I started to receive death notes from her, she wanted to kill me and you.

'This is one of the reasons I married your stepfather and came here to Europe. I knew no one would come here to find us, I felt we were safer far from Colombia, Brazil and that terrible situation I was in.

'When we were there, I received too many threats, and I reached the point where I couldn't cope anymore. It was difficult, but at the end of the day I took care of everything, and we are lucky to have had many people to help us in this process.

'Daniel, what I will say now will make you crazy, and the only thing I will ask you, is to take it easy, and think about it.' She took my hand and kissed it.

I couldn't answer, and just nodded, feeling my heart becoming heavy as a stone.

'I left Colombia and your father because I was afraid of what the future held for us. Even if we were all protected, I was still fearful for us.' She pressed my hand, and I asked, 'You told me my father was killed and that's why you escaped: what are you talking about?' She took a long sip of wine and looked into my eyes. 'No Daniel, you father was never killed, I escaped because I didn't want you to have a father and a future wrapped up in drugs and death.'

I felt numb, too much was happening, and the anger made my mind even foggier than before.

'Your father died a few weeks ago. For many years, he tried to reach us, but I didn't allow it. "Here."'

She took her laptop and passed it to me. '10 years ago, he found me, and from that point we started to reconnect again. He was still a trafficker, and had a new family. He wanted to meet me, but I was too afraid for us.'

I was deep in shock. I read through all their email exchanges quickly. His name was Daniel, and not the many other names my mother had invented in all those years. Then I stopped at an email that said, 'No Daniel, he died during birth.'

I looked at her in tears, 'Why?' My voice was broken.

She squeezed my hands tighter. 'Daniel, I couldn't allow him to take the only thing I love the most in this world. You are the son of love, and he didn't deserve to have you. I lied to him. I didn't want anything to happen to you, and it was better this way.'

I took my hands off hers. I was so angry. For all those years I had had a father, alive, and he thought I was dead. 'How can you say I was made with love, when you are telling me right now that for all these years you lied to both of us? How can you come here today, pretending I will be OK with what you are saying? He died, I never met him, and he never met me. You are fucked up.' I said.

'Daniel, please! You are just angry now, you don't understand. I did everything to protect us and have a future away from that madness.'

'And who told you this is the future I wanted? Who told you this is what I needed? All my life was fucked up because of your choices, and here I have the confirmation that you are so selfish you don't even care about people around you.' I was so angry that I broke the wine glass by throwing it on the floor.

'Daniel, calm down. You can't tell me now that you were interested in a man you never met. It was the right choice for all. He is now dead, and no one will bother us anymore. Come here.'

'Don't! Don't touch me. You had a choice, mother: you tried to protect us, all I see now is you trying to protect yourself with your martyrdom. I don't know how you can wake up each morning with all of these lies in your heart. You took away my chance to have a father,' I said.

'Son, I was your mother and father, and Josè was always there for you, you know that. You didn't need someone like this in your life.'

I took her glass and threw it on the floor. She stood up,

scared. I took her arm and said, 'Listen to me now. You are dead to me, and I don't feel ashamed of what I am saying. I don't hate you, but I am disgusted by you. It makes me sick to call you a mother, and you deserve to die. I will never talk to you, or to this family, again. If you ever try to call me again, I will sue you, and if Paloma tries to, I will ruin this family by telling everyone your truth: letting people know you are only interested in Josè's money, and nothing more. You have no son: delete me from your life.'

She screamed, crying, 'Daniel, please! You are just angry. I promise that from now on, everything will be different: I promise!' I moved my face closer to hers, and said, 'You are dead to me!' Then I left her there, went to my room, collected my things and left the house, with my mother screaming at the door, 'Please Daniel, don't go! We love you and we need you! We are a family.'

No! We were not a family, and we never had been.

That same day, I took a flight to London, and at the airport Roo and Frank were waiting for me.

Both gave me a hug, full of love. 'You are not alone.' Frank said, and he was right.

I am Daniel

Today is my 35th birthday.

What an achievement, for someone who has spent most of his life trying to destroy it. I spent most of my time waiting for people to accept and love me. And that made me forget the importance of being the king or the queen of my world. I gave my territory to many, allowing them to take pieces of me, leaving only emptiness and sadness to walk me through a journey that was not meant to be mine.

And healing, what a strange concept. When you walk out there, waiting to be healed, you don't realise one important thing. To be able to heal, you have first to learn who you truly are, what you want, and how strong you are when you have to face challenges. And the main challenge of all is life. Everything happens for a reason, people say. Yes, this is right, but you might add: 'everything happens for a reason because you choose for it to happen. Most of the time, we think the world is against us, but to be honest with you, the world is not against you, it is you that are against your own world.'

In the last five years, so many things have happened, and I have walked through my own journey aware of what I want, and how I want it to be.

When you are present with yourself, everything gets easier. Surely mistakes are always there to be made, but at the end of the day, every mistake is just a way for you to learn what you need, in order to survive and be yourself.

I survived many experiences and traumas. Some of them were so terrible that somehow I ask myself: how did I deal with it? And I have an answer for that: I was able, unconsciously, to listen to my inner voice.

Five years ago, I went back to therapy. After all my mother told me, and all the other things that had happened in my life, I needed help, but also someone who would make me understand that I should be able to accept myself first, making sure I am OK with my life.

And you know what is funny? In the past, I was diagnosed with Bipolar Disorder One, and five years later it came out, from many other tests and assessments, that I had what is called double personality syndrome, which came mainly from my childhood trauma, and the fact I tried so many times to use masks to cover my emotion and traumas, not just from the rest of the world, but mainly from myself.

So all of the drugs, alcohol and medicines were what I used to cover my reality. I tried for too long to conceal my problems, and that was not OK at all. In the end, I exploded.

I had choices and many solutions I could use, but I chose instead to mask my emotions, because that was the way I grew up. That was the way my mother taught me to live: 'Never show your weaknesses, just give the world what it wants from you. And the world doesn't want problems, only perfection.' In searching for perfection, we lose our truth. That is what I did, and that killed my spirit.

I was not ready for love at all. In fact, Simon, Jacob, Gabriel, and Thomas were great lovers, but also the worst. The worst because we grow up with a strange idea of love.

I think that movies, books, pornography, etc. has fucked up our idea of what we want from someone else. Add the fact that society silently says to us that without someone next to us, we are nothing. Everything around screams in our face that to be able to live a good life, you need someone by your side. In my case, they knew as much as I knew about love, and we crashed our castle, making it all so difficult to deal with.

I don't know much about male-female relationships, but I can say that in the gay community, it is more about showing up what we are not. For sure, not everyone in the community lives in this way, but all those meeting apps create big lions behind a screen, and then when we have someone in front of us, we don't know how to deal with it.

We live with a lack of confidence in what we really want, not to mention communication: we like to pretend. We are fearful of speaking out our truth.

In all those relationships, I allowed myself to become what they wanted me to be, but then there was a moment that I couldn't deal with it anymore, destroying not just the relationship, but also myself.

And that is the hardest part, because you have to deal with yourself 24/7, and if your lover is gone, you can't simply put yourself in the darkness, leaving all the problems there. We try, but in the end, the darkness comes to us, and we don't have any other choice but to deal with it.

In these five years, as I said before, many things have happened. Let me recap for you:

I moved back to London. Frank, Roo and I moved into the same house. It is important to always have people next to you who can support and give you strength every time you are in confusion.

After Farez's death, I stopped to ask myself many times if I was a good friend to him. I know in my heart I couldn't stop his death, but sometimes I think I could have done something to prevent it.

We were supportive of drugs, meaning we were high most of the time, and we influenced each other with that. We had big, deep useless conversations about life. We were young, innocent souls in a hell of a situation, trying to get attention from the world. And in all that self-searching, we used drugs as a sword against reality. That was our way to cover our fear of being lonely, and as much as we thought we had each other's backs, we both failed, falling constantly into the same pattern of mistakes.

We needed each other, and drugs were our link.

Back in London, I returned to my previous work in the second-hand vintage store. I decided that it was better for me to just be a sales assistant, and not a manager anymore. For most of my life, I had felt responsible for other people, and I didn't want that anymore, because I was not able to be responsible for myself, first and foremost.

I went back to my NA meetings, and sat there most of the time listening to people's experiences, giving hugs to those who felt alone in the process. Most of them were surprised by the gesture, but we all need to feel part of this world, don't we? And I want them to be part of this world too.

Eventually, I took a job at an East London magazine where I wrote about local events and the best places for drinks, lunches or dinners. That job helped me to connect better with people, to understand them and learn that we are all looking for something in life, and that by creating a strong community, we can achieve all of our life goals.

Frank, Roo and I went clubbing once a week. Each week, one of us would decide which club and event to be part of. In 2017, Sink the Pink was one of the best events in London. That collective had existed since 2008, but this was their big moment, and we were always going there dressing up in the most stupid and sexy way. There I learned about my gender and sexuality, acknowledging that for all my life I had lived with gender dysphoria without knowing what to call it.

I didn't feel like a man, and neither a woman, and at the same time I felt I was a man and sometimes a woman.

I learnt the meaning of being a GenderQueer, or fluid, in those nights out, sharing my experience with many other people living in a similar situation. I gave myself the opportunity to accept not just what was inside me, but also my body, attitude and behaviour. I started to learn what freedom meant, and I'm thankful for all the support I had in those days, and how that made me feel important enough to deal with my own persona.

I stayed in London for two more years, and then decided it was my time to leave the country and explore the world. I took a six-month sabbatical period and went travelling around Europe and then South America.

In South America, I went to Rio de Janeiro, the city I was born in. There I met Thiago, who became one of my best friends. We met by Copacabana Beach: he complimented my Amy Winehouse t-shirt, and from that point we started to talk and share many things we both loved to do. He took me to visit many places around Rio. There was nothing sexual between us, we were friends, and that was so magical that when I left Brazil for my next stop, we decided to tattoo *la figa*, which is a Brazilian good luck charm represented by a fist with a thumb between the index and middle finger. It was our ink connection, and we are still great friends today.

In spring 2019, I decided to go to the place where I had to resolve something I had avoided because of my fears.

I took my flight back to Madrid and from Madrid, I went back to Lanzarote.

In Lanzarote, I stayed in Haria first, and then called Antonio. He was so happy and surprised to hear me that he came to pick me up in Haria. He wanted me to go back to his house in La Graciosa, something I was OK with, but I was not sure how I would deal with Lucas' situation.

He told me on the journey that Lucas left the island many years before and went to live in El Hierro, another of the Canary Islands.

When I arrived at La Graciosa, I felt freedom and power, the same I had felt the first time I was there. Antonio gave me another of his houses, bigger than the previous one, with a little patio. He asked if it was OK for me to work for him, dealing with all the office work for his holiday home on the island and in Lanzarote: something I accepted instantly.

I won't lie to you, it was a big shock when I passed in front of Lucas' house. My heart stopped in front of that door. All our great moments together passed as a flash in my mind, and

I realised that I really loved Lucas and that love came from my heart, from my experience, and from us.

There was so much support in that relationship, that was something full of love. But at that time, I hadn't been ready for it. As much as I thought I was healed, I wasn't at all, and that messed up the only real honest relationship I had ever had.

That summer passed faster, and we had many tourists from all over the world. Frank and Roo came to visit me, and both fell in love with the island as well.

That August, I closed the biggest chapter of my life. My mother passed away from cancer. Paloma found out where I was, and came to the island to give me news. The only thing that came out of my mouth when she told me face to face was, 'My pain is gone and her pain too, I am happy she will be calm now.' She was speechless, she was probably waiting for another response, something more dramatic.

I wasn't sad about my mother's death: everyone dies. She had given me too much suffering, but that didn't mean much to me at that moment. I didn't hate her anymore, I just wanted to be free from her.

Paloma gave me a letter that my mother had written to me before her death. I took it and put it away in an old box. I already knew what was written there, I didn't want to deal with her victimhood even from death, so I eventually tore up the letter a few months ago: I didn't need to remember all the pain I had lived through with her.

Paloma also gave me a check with my share of the inheritance that I gave back to her, saying, 'Now, go and live your life freely.' She smiled, hugged me, and left.

From that day forward, we didn't connect to each other anymore, and that was the most respectful thing we could do for each other. I know it sounds harsh, but as I said, we live the way society tells us to behave, but that is not always what we really need. And deciding to not have a family member next to you is OK. We are taught that family is important, but what if it is not?

And then Christmas came. Antonio and his family invited me to stay with them in Lanzarote. It was a big Christmas party with family and friends, something I had never experienced before. It was such a great way to really feel the power of being loved, and part of a community.

We slept there, and the next day, we went back to La Graciosa, and by the door there was a big box waiting for me.

I was not expecting anything from anyone, because Frank, Roo and I had promised we would meet in Madrid in February and celebrate our special late Christmas.

I took the box inside the house. There wasn't any card with it, so I quickly opened it to find a painting.

It was a portrait of me in the middle of this wild landscape, signed by Lucas.

I was mesmerised, my heart beating went so fast I thought I would die. I was so scared, because I didn't know how I would be able to say sorry to Lucas for everything I'd done. After a while, someone knocked at the door.

I went to open it and in front of me was Lucas, with his curly dark hair, big white smile and a wild beard. 'Hey, Antonio said to me you were back, and I had this gift for you that I had been waiting to give to you for years.' My heartbeat raced. At that moment, I knew that the only person I wanted to be with was him.

2020 came, with all that pandemic craziness that put our lives on hold for many months.

Antonio passed away during that time. Unfortunately he caught that awful virus, and his body was not strong enough to cope with it.

He died on a rainy day. I think it was Mother Nature's way of saying how sorry she was, to lose such a great human being.

His death crushed everyone on the island like a big tsunami. No one was ready for that, as we are never ready when we are faced with death.

I stayed for the entire time close to his wife and family. During that evening, as a mourning moment, Antonio's friend played his favourite song on the guitar, in front of the white church of Nuestra Señora del Carmen, the only church on the island.

The sound of the guitar resounded all over the island: it was the most magical, but also the saddest moment we had ever experienced.

Antonio left his business to his wife, and his wife left it to me. They trusted me enough to keep the business as Antonio wanted. And, in April 2021, his wife decided to leave the island and move to Màlaga: she was too heartbroken to deal with her grief in a place where everything reminded her of her only love.

Each day, I lit a candle and spoke with Antonio, it was my way to feel him next to me. That became a routine, and somehow I felt he was there, giving me all the answers and tips I needed. He was not just a friend, but also a big brother and father to me, and not having him around was quite difficult to deal with, but I knew that he would have wanted me to be strong and happy.

Each day, I called his wife and shared gossip and business ideas. She was happy to have someone like me taking care of what they had created and dealt with for many years.

Summer 2021 was tough for the business. Many businesses in Lanzarote closed, and tourism was nothing compared to the years before. All the restrictions ruined so many people's businesses and dreams. I saw many places closing in Lanzarote and La Graciosa, and that broke my heart.

We still don't know how all this situation will affect us, things keep changing. Many of us have changed our attitude towards what we want, but many are angry and unsatisfied with the answers the world is giving us.

We were not ready for all that, as we are never ready to live life. But hey, we forget this part, thinking that destiny is there ready to give us something that will change our life, when in the end, we just need to build up what we want patiently, instead of trying to find a gateway to arrive at our goals faster.

All these years affected so much who I wanted to be, and now for the past year of my life, I begin to learn that nothing is forever, and we need to be ready for whatever will arrive, and adapt to the situation. I was too attached to what I thought I would never have, when in the end, all the tiny things and details were already present in my life. I just needed a kick in my ass to wake me up, something I gave to myself.

Many doors closed in front of me as many opened: many I closed because I was not ready to deal with myself and my problems.

We can have everything in life, but we can also lose everything in an instant, and for that, we should live life to the full, without being afraid of the outcome.

I was so afraid of not being loved, when at the end of the day, the only love I needed was my own love for myself. We are only able to be loved by the world when we are ready to love ourselves.

Today is my 35th birthday. I passed through so much shit that I should be broken in pieces right now, but let me say to you that I feel stronger than ever.

This morning, I woke up at 5 a.m., left the warmth of my bed and put on my swim trunks. Outside at that time it was chilly and windy, but I didn't care much: I just wanted to dip my body in the cold November ocean, something I do each morning, but today was special. I am 35 now, and as I thought, it was the best swim I had had in ages. I felt my body calm, clear and ready for this new chapter in my life.

I am now completely aware of what I want and what I don't want in my life.

For too many years, I was afraid of how the world would deal with my choices, and I can now drink a glass of wine without pushing myself into the darkness. I speak out loud about my emotions without being fearful of what the world will think about it. I accept the person I am, and I am learning that what I thought were my weaknesses are nothing more than my strongest part, and that it is amazing to be vulnerable in a world full of ego.

And if you ask me, 'do you regret your choices?' My answer is, 'No, I don't.' Every experience I've had was what I had to live through at that moment, was the best I could do to be able to survive the situation, and without them, I would not be the person I am today.

I am so glad to see the world with these new eyes, and fulfil myself with the power I create each day, when I wake up and I say to myself: 'you are doing great, you deserve yourself.'

I know now that happiness is not what they show us. It is not an expensive bag, car, or a big house. It is not money, as my mother taught me. Happiness is something more personal. It is what you choose and not what society asks you to be and have.

Happiness is me and what I build around me, making sure to be true to my emotions without masking them with things I don't need anymore.

And now I am here, writing these pages for you. In front of me, the ocean, with its waves crashing the coast, the sky sunny, with the wind moving the sand and palm trees outside. In the background, Florence and the Machine singing:

'But I must confess I did all for myself, I gathered you here to hide from some vast unnameable fear. But loneliness never left me, I always took with me, but I can put it down in the pleasure of your company ....' Hector is on the floor next to my feet, playing gently with his favourite toy. On the wall to my left, the portrait Lucas gifted me, and many other paintings he created over the years.

On the table, the flowers I've received from my neighbours, and an empty white cup of tea I left this morning after I dipped my soul in the ocean. On my right, Lucas with a sleepy face, smiling and opening his arms, ready to hug me:

'*Amor*, happy birthday, I love you!'

Yes, happy birthday to me.

Acknowledgements

The following chapters take their titles from songs by Florence + the Machine, as detailed below:

'Hurricane Drunk' — Album *Lungs* (2009)
'Long & Lost' — Album *How Big, How Blue, How Beautiful* (2015)
'What the Water Gave Me'— Album *Ceremonials* (2011)
'Various Storms & Saints' — Album *How Big, How Blue, How Beautiful* (2015)
'My Boy Builds Coffins' — Album *Lungs* (2009)
'Seven Devils' — Album *Ceremonials* (2011)
'Light Of Love' — Single (2020)
'Ghosts' — Album *Lungs* (2009)
'Mother' — Album *How Big, How Blue, How Beautiful* (2015)
'Heaven Is Here'— Album *Dance Fever* (2022)
'Cosmic Love' — Album *Lungs* (2009)
'Ship to Wreck' — Album *How Big, How Blue, How Beautiful* (2015)
'Kiss with a Fist' Album *Lungs* (2009)

Also Available From EIF

(via Amazon and in selected bookstores)

Archery in the UK**
by Nick Reeves and Ingrid Wilson**

ISBN: 9781739757786

Inspired by the Lyrical Ballads of Wordsworth and Coleridge, two authors set out to pen a contemporary homage to this timeless collection. As the collaboration progresses, however, the poetry and the unique narrative it carries takes on a life of its own. Thus, the authors come to tell their story through a collection of ballads, sonnets, pantoums and other forms: under arches, over bridges and against the backdrop of the fabled Northlands: from Tyne and Wear to Cumbria and beyond.

40 Poems At 40**
by Ingrid Wilson**

ISBN: 9781739757700

40 Poems is the debut poetry collection from Ingrid Wilson. It is poetry of place and space, and here lie the clues and the beauty to Wilson's poetry. Her work is charted, landscaped, travelled, explorative and laden with adventure. There are bright, sad, dreamy postcards telling of the beauty of Barcelona, the slate-grey, but singing, county of Cumbria, Malaga, 'the emptiness' of Manchester, 'the fields' of London, 'the ancient pasts' of Newcastle, the mysterious beauty of Slovenia, Venice and its lullaby… lapping water is never far from her ear.

A reflective, rich debut that reveals, in startling images and with dextrous word-play, a trove for those of us learning to live and to love.

Wounds I Healed: The Poetry of Strong Women
edited by Gabriela Marie Milton

ISBN: 9781739757724

Award-winning authors, Pushcart nominees, emerging poets, voices of women and men, come to the fore in this stunning, powerful, and unique anthology. These poems testify both to the challenges that women face in our society, and to their power to overcome them. A memorable collection of over 200 poems by more than 100 authors, this anthology is a must-have for all lovers of poetry. We all can benefit from the poetry of survival, and of healing. We all can benefit from the experiences so beautifully evoked in this book. We can all come together to emerge triumphant from pain.

Nature Speaks of Love and Sorrow
by Jeff Flesch

ISBN: 9781739757755

In this hotly-anticipated debut poetry collection from Jeff Flesch, the author invites us to take a voyage with him through trauma and pain into acceptance and bliss in the embrace of nature itself. Jeff's poems are infused with the textures and colours of the natural world, and his journey through this sensory paradise provides the backdrop to his inner journey towards healing and growth.

Three-Penny Memories, A Poetic Memoir
by Barbara Harris Leonhard

ISBN: 9781739757762

"*Do you love your mother?*"
— This provocative question provides the catalyst for this stunning poetic memoir from Barbara Harris Leonhard. Through her artfully-crafted poetry, the author considers where her love and loyalties lie following her aging mother's diagnosis with Alzheimer's.

Due for release 20 May 2023:

Re-create and Celebrate: 7 Steps to turn your Dreams into Reality
by Cindy Georgakas

ISBN: 9781739404413

In this unique book, Cindy guides her readers through simple steps to achieve the life they have always dreamed of. Not simply life goals, but a whole new outlook and way of living. Through her transformational techniques and practices, which she has gained from decades of experience in the field of life coaching, she provides a teaching memoir and workbook containing the tools to build a blueprint to a life of fulfillment, inner peace and happiness.